Praise for

The Best Place to Be

"Virginia Woolf meets Candace Bushnell in these funny, beautifully written linked stories."

—*Elle* Reader's Prize

"Following Grace through the maze of midlife and youth . . . is a journey that is smack-your-forehead familiar, and so crazily funny you could cry."

—*O, The Oprah Magazine*

"Dormen's stories are often delightfully, crushingly funny."

—Alex Kuczynski, *The New York Times Book Review*

"Dormen's . . . conversational short stories . . . read like the best kind of personal essays: dispatches from the (not all bad) front."

—*More* magazine

"Researching an article called 'Is This Man Marriage Material?' she remembers, ' "What about a man who isn't sure what an emotion is?" had been one of my questions. Then I described a man not unlike the man I was then dating, my future husband, a man who thought tired was a feeling.' As I calculate the weight of most current fiction, this sentence tips the scales."

—*The Boston Globe*

"[Grace] calls her own bluff and steps deftly around self-pity as if it were a broken place in the sidewalk."

—Julia Keller, *Chicago Tribune*

"A beautifully realized collection of linked short stories."

—*The Hartford Courant*

"Dormen's high-performance writin͏͏ formula one racer, time travels like V

"Dormen writes adeptly and winning.

—*The Palm Beach Post*

"Essays are waiting to be written about how Dormen deals with the dark side of 12, compared to, say . . . Nabokov."

—Juliet Waters, *Montreal Mirror*

"In Dormen's accomplished collection . . . [her] narrator takes plenty of knocks, making the happiness she finds all the sweeter."

—*Publishers Weekly*

"Emerging writer Dormen's engaging fiction moves at a fluid pace with an equally affecting sense of poignancy and humor."

—*Booklist*

"Whether she's spending Thanksgiving in Rome watching reruns of the Kennedy assassination, trying to talk her mother out of her face lift fund so she can pay down her credit card debt, interviewing marriage counselors in Starbucks, or trying to outsmart her larcenous housekeeper, Grace Hanford's life makes perfect postmodern sense. *The Best Place to Be* is smart, funny, and completely delightful; it's going to make a lot of readers very happy."

—Kathryn Harrison, author of *Envy* and *The Kiss*

"Lesley Dormen's funny, bittersweet tale is the knowing portrait of a particular yet archetypal modern woman caught between the demands of her family and her personal ambitions. What captivated me most, however, was the shadow portrait in these pages: a fine cameo of millennial New York, rendered with the same sly, satiric affection that Steve Martin lavished on Los Angeles in *Shopgirl*."

—Julia Glass, author of *Three Junes* and *The Whole World Over*

"*The Best Place to Be* is a terrific debut. Smart, funny, wise, and altogether heartening. These linked stories read like dispatches from the front of modern womanhood. Lesley Dormen has crafted this book so carefully and elegantly that you might not notice how beautifully it's written. Notice. She's the real deal."

—Dani Shapiro, author of *Slow Motion* and *Black and White*

The Best Place to Be

LESLEY DORMEN

Simon & Schuster Paperbacks
New York London Toronto Sydney

SIMON & SCHUSTER PAPERBACKS
A Division of Simon & Schuster, Inc.
1230 Avenue of the Americas
New York, NY 10020

Five of these stories were previously published in slightly different form as follows: "The Old Economy Husband" in *The Atlantic Monthly*; "Curvy" in *Ploughshares*; "I Asked My Mother" in *Five Points*; "Gladiators" in *Open City*; "The Best Place to Be" in *Glimmer Train*.

First Simon & Schuster trade paperback edition April 2008

SIMON & SCHUSTER PAPERBACKS and colophon are registered trademarks of Simon & Schuster, Inc.

For information about special discounts for bulk purchases, please contact Simon & Schuster Special Sales at 1-800-456-6798 or business@simonandschuster.com

Designed by Andrea C. Uva

Manufactured in the United States of America

10 9 8 7 6 5 4 3 2 1

The Library of Congress has cataloged the hardcover edition as follows:

Dormen, Lesley
        The best place to be / Lesley Dormen.
             p. cm.
        I. Title.
    PS3604.O75B47 2007
    813'.6—dc22

                                        2006050184

ISBN-13: 978-1-4165-3261-3
ISBN-10:   1-4165-3261-7
ISBN-13: 978-1-4165-3262-0 (pbk)
ISBN-10:   1-4165-3262-5 (pbk)

This book is for Quentin

Contents

The Old Economy Husband 1

Figure of a Woman 23

Curvy 43

The Secret of Drawing 69

I Asked My Mother 103

Gladiators 109

General Strike 123

The Best Place to Be 155

The Best Place to Be

The Old Economy Husband

It was that summer, the summer we were fifty and the little Cuban boy went home to no mother, not the first West Nile virus summer but the second, the Hillary and *Survivor* summer, you know that summer, the summer the women were manhandled in the park and the kids lined up for Harry Potter, the summer we were fifty, all of us, fifty and holding, the ones a little older and the ones a little younger, fifty and holding, like thirty and holding only fifty, and it was summer and the ones who were rich were and the ones who weren't weren't but we were all fifty, every one of us, and holding.

We were in the city that summer because we couldn't afford a vacation and we couldn't afford a beach house, because our oven died and it was vintage

1929 or something and connected to the dishwasher in some complicated way having to do with converted residential hotels—in other words irreplaceable—and one thing led to another and now we had twenty thousand dollars' worth of European-made appliances on order. It was the summer we renovated the kitchen.

"Will you call the Miele place in the morning?" I asked Richard. "Will you remember to because I can't face it. Will you?" Our contractor was useless. Also he was in Brazil.

"I'll do it," Richard said. "I said I would."

"Because you have to, sweetie, okay?" What was I, deaf? He said he would.

One minute I was disgusted with myself for owning a fancy dishwasher I couldn't even pronounce—Meal? Mee-lay? May-lay?—the next I was in a rage over the incompetence of the people responsible for getting it to me. Those were the two ways I was.

Everything that used to be in the kitchen was spread out all over the living room—one thing about a renovation was you saw all the stuff you never used with sickening clarity, the useless stupid juice glasses and the dust-encrusted early-eighties cappuccino maker and the rusted flour sifter and the grimy oven mitts from the Caribbean vacations, cartons of junk you dragged guiltily down the hall to the recycling room for the building staff to pick over. The bathroom was now the acting kitchen and a lot of stuff that used to be in the living room, specifically the dining room, was in my office.

We ate dinner there, in front of the TV. It was summer so there was nothing on. We were watching a biography of the actress Jane Seymour, Dr. Quinn, with the hair. How her first husband left her and her life was terrible, then she had a baby, then her life was terrible again, then she had another baby. Like that. Terrible, baby, terrible, baby, commercial, baby, baby, with some husbands thrown in and a castle and the hair.

Richard carried our dirty dinner dishes to the bathroom—it was his week to cook and like a champ he'd brought in takeout burritos—and reappeared with dessert, from somewhere, on plates: pie. He kissed the top of my head. "Do you know that you're my fave?" he said. He said it a lot lately, probably picking up those voodoo vibes of double-dose Zoloft, of Tylenol PM addiction, of night-sweaty breakdown. Those crazy fifty-year-old women! He said "You're my fave" instead of "I love you" instead of "Take whatever hormone you want just don't get cancer" instead of "I'm sorry I already had children in my first marriage and didn't want any in my second and you didn't get to be a mother." Fine. He wasn't exactly sorry, but it was fine anyway. He was my fave, too. That was me, married to the one man who made me feel like my fiercest, most clear-hearted twelve-year-old self and not any of the men who made me feel that other way, that euphorically grandiose, desperately insecure, wildly libidinous twenty-five-year-old way.

We ate the pie.

Dr. Quinn was looking back, saying it was all

worth it. I picked up the pie plates, headed for the bathroom, and considered walking straight out the door and shoving everything down the compactor. Throwing out was definitely doing it for me lately. I made a few mistakes: our income tax files from 1990 to 1995, a set of Berlitz tapes (French), the zip-in lining to Richard's raincoat. But why tell him now, when it was only July and he wouldn't need the coat until November. If I were a mother, my kids could be grown and gone by now. Or they could be triplets about to turn three. Or murdered or run over or autistic or kidnapped or cancer-riddled and bald or schizophrenic or in prison or nanny-shaken or searching for their real mother or late getting home from school. At least I'd been spared that, that's what I told myself, because I knew I'd never survive that, any of that, not a chance.

That was my first summer on earth as an orphan. Wasn't that every kid's fantasy? Well, it had been mine. I loved the Hayley Mills *Biography*. *The Parent Trap* was a great movie. My mother died last spring. I was used to my father being dead—he died three years ago and I barely knew him. Now I was fifty, not a mother, not a daughter, and the kitchen was in the living room and I didn't know how I was supposed to behave.

We went to bed, Richard instantly asleep and making those putt-putt noises. I bounced around violently a few times, blew softly into his ear, huffed off to the living room sofa for a read, came back to bed and by then he'd quieted down. I fell asleep with my book open. At some point Richard woke, bookmarked my page, turned out my light, nuzzled my lips with my bite guard until I put it in.

He was long and lanky, my husband, as straight-arrow decent as Jimmy Stewart. Not neurotic or tricky, not the least bit mean. He'd never taken a drug, not even pot. "Are you sure you're even an American?" I asked him. He never got pissed off at me, just came home with that open look on his face, now and then passing on stories about his temper—losing it with the poky old people in the supermarket checkout line, with the virago in the laundry room who took his still wet clothes out of the dryer, with the punk who threatened him on a streetcorner. When he cupped my head with his hand while we made love, I was startled all over again at the largeness of it, at what a man's hand can be, and I liked it, those big fingers twining my hair, I really liked it a lot, that largeness. I just kept forgetting how much I liked it, sexual memory malaise, like one of those eccentrically damaged Oliver Sacks people who couldn't remember a conversation beyond five minutes ago. The Woman Who Couldn't Retain the Memory of Pleasure. Doesn't every marriage contain its own evil twin? Maybe I was ours. Maylay, Mai Lai, malaise.

In the morning, Richard made the coffee in the bathroom and we asked each other how we slept and read the *Times*.

I was happy to get out of the apartment. Besides the money, it was why I took the job ghostwriting Winston Winter's book on etiquette. Three days a week I took the bus from lower Fifth Avenue to Winston Winter Lifestyles on upper Madison Avenue. Winston was Manhattan's most famous party and wedding planner. Today we were working on Chapter Seven: How to Raise a Gracious Child.

I'd always made a decent living as a magazine writer. My specialty was sex and dating, the five-friend, two-shrink service piece dissecting the romantic lives of single women in their twenties and thirties and, occasionally, in their early forties though not in any of the unmentionable decades after that, for *Marvelous Woman* magazine. I even wrote a column for single women called "By Yourself." Then one day I realized that I couldn't write another word on that subject. What else was there to say? How could I ask one more woman or one more representative for women what was going right or wrong in her life, what she wanted that she didn't have, what she wound up getting even though she had never claimed to want it and never asked for it. I couldn't even bear to read any more articles about women's lives, especially the serious ones written by the very smartest women that showed irrefutably all that remained wrong with women and the culture that served women despite everyone's best intentions and efforts. I couldn't bear thinking, Yes! Exactly! My brains hurt from nodding my head in so much agreement.

"Just do what you want for a while. We'll dip into the nest egg if we have to," Richard said when I told him how adrift I felt. He was an Old Economy husband.

He never wanted to dip into the nest egg, ever. His willingness to dip into it now alarmed me. Was now the time for the dipping to begin? And if now wasn't the time, when was the time? I asked him again to explain the financial strategy of investing for the long haul.

"Isn't the haul getting shorter by the minute?" I said.

"Well, that's one way to look at it," he said.

I said no the first time Winston Winter Lifestyles asked me to write the etiquette book. Ghostwriter? Way too beside the point—whatever the point was. They said, "You don't understand! It's not just a guide to etiquette! It's a guide to the new spiritual etiquette!" Then they offered me a little bit more money, enough to make their original offer feel that much more insulting. I've noticed that people tend to offer you things when you say no to them, one more important lesson I've learned too late in life for it to do me any good. Didn't I have to earn *some* money? I mean, I'd never *not* earned money. Richard's salary had already taken a dive. After years of Wall Street money-managing, he was handling finances for a small foundation. He had an office high up in the Empire State Building. What about haircuts? Was the nest egg expected to pay for those? What about long-term-care insurance? Not to mention the looming face-lift expense. I was beginning to suspect that the whole thing was careering toward some horrifying endgame in which people behaved either well or badly, in which strategies either panned out or didn't pan out, in which being a person with good bone structure meant one thing and truly understanding what it means to forgive and forget meant something else. I didn't know what I wanted to do. I wanted to train a golden retriever puppy to be a working companion for the handicapped, then weep when the time came to turn the dog over to its grateful new owner.

Maybe it would be good for me to take on an ego-less project, I told myself. That way I'd make some money and empty myself at the same time, create room for something new, something meaningful. Not that etiquette was meaningless. Even the rudest people expressed outrage at the revolting treatment they received from others. No, etiquette was meaningful.

There might be travel involved, Winston's people added, and they pointed out that Winston Winter Lifestyles had an arrangement with the Four Seasons Hotel. Some exquisitely brought-up underling must have recalled me mentioning in a meeting that I had found the beds in that hotel chain to be the only beds I could sleep on without taking a ten-milligram Ambien first. I said okay, I would do it.

Richard left for work. I watched for him from the window, and when he reached the corner I waved, adding a manic shimmy to make him laugh. An hour later, I collected my stuff and walked to the bus stop at University Place and Ninth Street, directly in front of the sexy lingerie boutique. I loved my neighborhood. I'd lived in it for over twenty years, half of those years the tail end of my long single-woman life, a drama played out just a few blocks adjacent to where I lived now. Every time I left the house I saw overlapping pieces of my present and my past: the dead-in-the-water blind dates, the still married ex-lover, former colleagues and current shopkeepers, the assortment of nodding-acquaintance neighbors. Once I saw the Pope pass by in his Popemobile. I'd lived here long enough to see my UPS man go completely gray.

A dozen tiny day campers on a leash drifted past Bagel Bob's. When I first moved to Greenwich Village, I never saw a single infant or toddler on the street. Where were all the families? Maybe on the Upper West Side. I was a suburban girl, transplanted to the city on the morning after the sexual revolution. Those were the days when you slept with every man who so much as caught your eye across a party. I tumbled desperately in and out of love. When love appeared, I stopped worrying about my future—only to be thrown into teeth-grinding uncertainty when it vanished. One day, without warning, the new mothers appeared. They blanketed the sidewalks like startling spring snow, pale, dazed and puffy-eyed, bravely lipsticked, their babies in a pouch. But it was the mothers who looked newborn.

When the bus swung over to the curb, I climbed on along with three bus-specific women, capable widows with decorative brooches and sensible shoes. The bus was so civilized. I settled into a window seat, and we bullied our way toward Union Square. At Park Avenue South it turned north and began making stops again. By the time we began the crawl up Madison Avenue, there was standing room only.

I saw Winston Winter on *Oprah* once. He was explaining how to plan a wedding that included white doves, Byzantine place settings, robed choirs, and chandeliers made from the petals of orchids bred for that purpose. Apparently even ordinary Americans now wanted weddings that resembled papal investiture ceremonies from the fourteenth century or replicas of the exact wedding that Celine Dion had. On television Winston Winter appeared suntanned and buoyant, with very white teeth and an accent I couldn't place but that I recognized from Merchant-Ivory films.

I'd never imagined that sort of wedding for myself. I'd never imagined any sort of wedding, really, never pictured myself a bride at all. My single life was staged in a tiny studio apartment that often felt like a waiting room for marriage, but the Big White Day never seized my imagination as the denouement I was waiting *for*. The story I was in seemed more closely based on the disease model. I had turned out to be one of those women for whom the virus of infatuation—fever and delirium followed by a wasting, nineteenth-century-like decline, then protracted convalescence—was potentially lethal. At best the virus became latent, resurfacing as New Year's Eve Disease and other nuisance ailments. I noticed that some women had theories about men that, if not a cure, seemed to shorten the illness: Men were childish, men were selfish, men were insecure. Others relied on talismans and folklore, the equivalent of hanging garlic around your neck: Never prepare a cheese tray for a first date; always answer the door without your shoes on; when he calls, announce that you just got out of the shower.

"Men like women who are full of life!" my mother offered—somewhat disingenuously, I thought, since we both knew it was the virus's cunning to mimic that feeling.

I didn't have any theories. To me men were the great mystery, the source of all pleasure and pain. I admired them as poets—the way they described a woman as having a "thin waist," the dress she wore as "sort of greenish." Lacking language for unnamed experience, men were forced to invent it. "If no one else is President, why can't I be President until the new one gets elected?" a lover with whom I wanted to break up once said. Another, on his way out the door, explained that he always found himself "Slip-Sliding Away."

I realized I'd better get some theories. I was still working on it when Richard wandered into the middle of my love affair with a not-quite-divorced alcoholic Egyptian diplomat. I still didn't know how I managed to choose happiness—I barely recognized it. Richard and I married, eventually, in our own home and with the smallest amount of hoopla. That became my theory, but only retrospectively: You can choose.

At Thirty-third Street, the bus passed the hotel where my father and his wife stayed the time he came to New York, long before I met Richard. I was thirty-five then and had seen my father only a few times. My mother had divorced him when I was six, remarrying twice more

11

after that, never happily. My father seemed gentle and kind. I asked him two questions. "Do you think I'm pretty?" and "If you had one question to ask me, what would it be?" He said he did think I was pretty, that I looked like my mother. His question was: Why aren't you married?

Three years ago his wife phoned to say he'd had a stroke. Did I want to come? I flew to Cleveland. My father was in Intensive Care, in a coma. I stood by his bed and held his hand. I repeated his name. "Irv? Irv?" And "Can you hear me? If you can hear me, squeeze my hand." Those were the only words I knew to say at the bedside of a comatose person. His wife stood on the other side of the hospital bed and held his other hand. She looked over at me benignly. "Grace," his wife said, "why don't you try calling him Dad?" It turned out not to be like a scene from a Golden Age of MGM movie at all, more like a scene from a Lifetime Original Movie. I didn't want to be rude. But when I tried substituting the word "Dad" for "Irv," my father still didn't answer and he still didn't squeeze my hand. I flew back to New York the same day.

All the parents were dying, the decent ones and the nightmares, the incest parents and the saints, the parents who doted and the ones who drank, the parents who lied and the parents who beat you up, the parents who always preferred your younger sister older brother dog, the silent fathers and the shopping mothers, the adulterous parents and the religious nuts, the ones who came to every game forgot to pick you up at the movies bought you the wrong birthday present didn't give you piano lessons made you try out for band, the ones who didn't notice you were gifted depressed gay fat thin suicidal talented bulimic and the ones who did. Who would be left to remember World War II and the cha-cha and the thank-you note? Yes, the end of Communism was huge. But the end of parents! I went to a funeral just a few weeks ago, the father of a friend. They had an open casket. A woman standing in front of it took out her cell phone and made a call.

At Forty-second and Madison, roughly halfway to Winston's, I gave up my seat to an elderly man, then was jostled—a surprising rudeness—as I grabbed for the pole. The tricky blocks were ahead, the blocks that bordered my mother's neighborhood, the restaurants where we met for lunch, the office buildings where we went for her doctors' appointments. Although my mother had held on to her glamour almost to the end, glaucoma had demanded certain compromises: rubber-soled shoes and minimal makeup. Every six weeks we went to the ophthalmologist. I sat with her in the darkened examining room while the ancient, elegant Dr Berg checked her eye pressure. My mother's feet, once snappy in sling-backs, sat meekly on the footrest like those of an obedient kindergartner, in Reeboks and slipping-down socks. A few months before she died, we went for an MRI. By then my mother thought she was being kept against her will at a spa, one where the guests had scarily whitened faces. "Do you have a locker here, too?" she asked me in a polite voice. I didn't know what to say. Who would know what to say? What was the right thing to say? A cell phone at a casket was clear. Everything else was up for grabs. The MRI room was as noisy as any Manhattan construction site. I removed my watch and my wedding band, as instructed, and sat on a folding chair at one end of the tunnel, holding my mother's foot as she disappeared inside. I wondered who would hold my foot.

Abby was the person with whom I regularly shared Winston's etiquette advice. Abby had been my editor at *Marvelous Woman*. "The man is irony-proof," Abby often said in a reverent voice. She owned all of Winston's books. She was right. Everything about Winston was unironic. Abby was particularly taken with Winston's dictum about the proper moment to pick up your fork and begin eating your meal at a dinner party. "Once three or four plates are served, you may begin," Winston said. "A gracious host or hostess doesn't want any of her guests to eat food that has grown cold." "Really? He said that?" Abby seemed as surprised to hear this as Richard had been when I told him that Warren Beatty and Shirley MacLaine were brother and sister.

I wrote my first article for Abby, on contraception etiquette. It was while doing research for it that I came across Emily Post's Rules for Debutantes. My mother had given me a copy of Emily Post's *Etiquette* when I graduated from high school. I had dutifully moved that book from shelf to shelf over the decades since without ever once opening it. How was I to know that hidden away in that seemingly useless volume were three rules containing all the guidance any young woman would ever need? Abby and I quoted them to each other regularly: *Do not lean on anyone for support unless necessary. Do not allow anyone to paw you. On no account force yourself to laugh.* Emily Post didn't cover contraception etiquette.

I got off the bus at Seventy-ninth Street and walked the few blocks to Winston's apartment. They were the same elegantly proportioned blocks I used to travel to when I was seeing my former psychotherapist, Dr. Isabella Gold. Week after week, year after year, I carried individual dreams from my apartment to Dr. Gold's office, dream by dream, one dream at a time, as if my job were to transfer an entire universe of matter from one place to another by teaspoonful. Then one day the work was done. All of the matter that had been in one place was now in another place entirely and I couldn't picture or imagine what used to be in either place. That was New York in a nutshell, I realized. Things changed all the time. As soon as the change was complete, it was impossible to reconstruct the past. It couldn't be done. The former landscape would always feel like a dream or a lie.

Winston's building was small and elegant, with a long green canopy and an elevator man. The first time I came here, the elevator man repeated, "Winston Winter!" and took me to the eleventh floor. When the doors opened I found myself in a small red-lacquered jewelbox of an entryway, with an umbrella holder, a gilt mirror, and two doors. One door led to the living quarters of the apartment, the other door to the office quarters. "Have a good day!" the elevator man said and left me there. I couldn't remember which door I had been told to knock on. I began to break into a bit of a sweat. It reminded me of a brain-teaser my husband liked: Twins confined in a tower room with two doors. One door leads to freedom, the other to the executioner. One twin tells the truth, the other twin lies. Ask one twin one question to determine the door to freedom. What question? Which twin? That to me seemed to sum up everything.

As it turned out, it didn't matter which door I knocked on because no one heard me. Eventually the housekeeper, Margaret, wandered out with the recyclables and let me in. "Oh, he's so late, my boss!" she said. "Juice?" Then she pointed toward a room with walls the color of eggplant and I went in and sat down on a burnt-orange velvet sofa. Winston shouted from another room, "Give her some of that mango pango juice!" Occasionally he sang out an order to an assistant whose name was either Patricia or Felicia or Delicious. "Navy taffeta for the tables! And four dozen candelabra!" While I waited for Winston, I tried identifying the wonderful scent of the candle burning on the wenge wood table and attempted to add up how much everything in that one room cost and began to feel downhearted about my own apartment with its deficiency of silver cigarette boxes and thirties cocktail accessories. Why hadn't I thought of eggplant as a color?

Today the door was open and I walked right in. Felicia Delicious was doing something with bubble wrap. "Good morning, Grace. How are you this morning?" She was twenty-three tops. I wanted to throw my arms around her.

"Gracie, my love! Just finishing up the morning's e-mail. Get comfy, darling." Winston was seated at his Art Deco desk, laptop open. He wore narrow pants and the thinnest summer cashmere pullover, both the color of slate, and on his feet were exquisite objects that seemed to be the marriage of an athletic shoe and a Ferrari. His face looked as if it had just returned from Sardinia.

I put my microcassette recorder on the table and opened my notebook. I wrote down everything Winston said in case of tape malfunction.

He came around to the sofa, kissed me on both cheeks, and settled into one corner. "So where are we today, my sweet?"

"We're beginning Chapter Seven," I said. "How to Raise a Gracious Child." Oh boy. Winston Winter on child-rearing.

"Very important! A topic dear to my heart. Because you know, Grace, good manners begin with children. Margaret! Mango pango on a tray, please, thank you! With instilling respect and integrity and compassion. With setting limits."

I smiled. That was my interviewing technique. I wrote down the words "respect, integrity, compassion."

Winston lifted his exfoliated chin and sniffed the unironic air.

"Let's see . . . a section on those vile people who let their children run up and down the aisle of airplanes . . . Should we talk about physical punishment now or at the end?"

"I think it's probably best to stick to etiquette," I said. "Like, should you bring your kid to a dinner party. Only because, well, that's more your area, right?"

"Never strike your child in anger."

I wrote it down.

He hit Pause while Margaret set down a tray with juice. "What about you, Grace? Do you and your husband plan on having children? Thank you, Margaret, lovely." I felt oddly invisible. How old did this man think I was? Did I register on him at all?

At lunchtime, we sat on tall stools in the handsome stainless steel and wood kitchen eating Margaret's vegetable soup while Winston oversaw the cutting and arranging in various-sized vases of that day's delivery of orange roses. During Chapter Four: An Organized Home Is a Spiritual Home, Winston had opened his kitchen cabinets and bedroom closets—spices alphabetic, Prada white to black—and discussed his philosophy of creating a peaceful environment. "Edit! Edit! Edit!" During Chapter Six: Positive Energy in Difficult Situations, Winston addressed the etiquette of blame. "Let it go!" Every chapter seemed to have an etiquette situation capable of being resolved by "Send a fragrant candle!"

It was close to five when Winston and I finished up. I walked to the subway, feeling perfectly empty.

18

Walking down the stairs, plucking my MetroCard from where I'd stuck it inside a book, I sensed the absence of something. I took the local to Union Square and when I got off and had walked up the stairs and onto the corner of Broadway, I stopped. I rummaged through my bag. It was my wallet that was gone. Uncomprehending grief swam through my bloodstream. Then it swam out. I remembered: There was an 800 number at home, I had all my account numbers stored on my computer, I could replace my driver's license by mail. My legs moved again, and I walked toward home.

In the window of the coffee shop on University Place and Twelfth Street, I saw the two ancient sisters seated in their customary window booth having the early-bird dinner. Both women had snowy hair and the tactful, pensive face of Miss Marple. I was always struck by how complex and subtle a variation each sister was on the other—the piled white hair, the parchment skin, the casually worn quirky piece of jewelry, the comfortably inward expressions—and by how deeply at home each sister appeared to be in the other's company. That's me and Abby, I always thought, when the husbands are dead. I wished that I knew everything about those sisters and their lives. Who had they loved and what had their little piece of New York looked like back at the beginning and which small luxuries had fallen away and which did they still cling to? Were they still moving forward or content to hang on? That was the mystery.

When I got home, I tried not to look at the boxes, at the gaping empty kitchen, at the living room mess. I went

19

straight to my office and called American Express, and the bank, and then Abby, because you had to say out loud, "My wallet was stolen." I remembered the lengthy recovery time these routine losses exacted when I was twenty-five and thirty, the doomed sense that keys and credit cards and salad-bar coupons were not only irreplaceable but ominous metaphors for everything bad to come. But by the time my apartment was burglarized at thirty-five, I'd come to know the losses bluntly for what they were: stuff you missed and, eventually, replaced, even though you never got back exactly what you'd lost. Then I spoke out loud to the quiet apartment. "Mom," I said. I said it again. Then I flung open the hall closet and threw out every cheap umbrella I could get my hands on.

Being fifty give or take was like being an original Supreme. Some later groups could call themselves the Supremes, they could sing "Baby Love," but we were the one-and-onlys. And that was also our curse. Because no experience we had in our lives could be unique. There would be a brief window during which we naively thought we were having a unique experience—laughing at Steve Martin, eating sushi, forgetting the word for fear-of-leaving-the-house—and then that window would close. Five minutes later everyone would be claiming that experience. That experience would be on the cover of *Newsweek* and people we had the deepest contempt for would be selling miniseries based on it. Everyone's parents were going to die, even the parents of those middle-aged celebrities with twenty-five-year-old skin who paid Winston Winter to plan birthday parties for their toddler triplets.

It was close to seven when someone phoned from Billy's Topless, a bar on Sixth Avenue. My wallet was there, emptied of cash, but with credit cards in it. I said thank you, and that I'd come and pick it up, and thank you again.

Richard called just after that. How was I? I said I was fine and told him all about Winston and the wallet. I stood at the window talking to him like that, about my day, watching the midsummer sky turn to dusk. I could see Richard's office building from the window where I stood. The sky turned a deep navy as we talked, and then it was night, and the building's upper stories blazed with light. When I concentrated and counted carefully, I was able to find exactly where Richard was, up on the eightieth floor. We knew we had a spectacular view when we moved into our apartment, but we'd always seen it in daylight. Not until our first night there did we really know how lucky we were.

We talked a little more that way, me at home staring out the window, Richard gathering up his things before heading home. We made dinner plans. "Ready?" Richard said then.

"Yep."

He switched to the speakerphone. Then he flickered the lights in his office, on and off, on and off. One, two, three blinks.

"Can you see them?" he called out. "Can you see them now?"

I could, I could see them, an improbable mile away, at not quite the top, a narrow band of flickering lights.

"Yes!" I said. "I can see them!" What were the odds of such a thing in such a city? What were the odds? I remembered how happy I was. I was just happy.

Figure of a Woman

*M*en *and women.* Men and women. And restaurants. My friend Phoebe sits at a small round cocktail table before a plate of fried zucchini heaped like Lincoln Logs. Her ginger hair, unstyled, falls in waves and frizzles to small square shoulders. Her back is absolutely straight, a stoic's back. Her breasts are loose and full inside a crayon-red corduroy dress, feet tucked up Indian-style, strappy shoes in a tangle on the floor. Those pale blue eyes and freckles. That serious challenging child's face. Only her eyes signal the waiter. "A tortellini appetizer," she says.

It's one of those nights, those nights of eating out with married people. Night after night after night. Phoebe and me. Phoebe and Paul and me.

"Don't you think Grace looks pretty tonight?"

It's Phoebe still married to Paul and starting to say stuff like—well, that. It's a triangle, smudgy around the edges, but a triangle, no question. Am I not the expert? Yes, I am a geometry genius, and this is my prime.

Rob, Steve, Mitch, Richard: Blind dates past, present, future. We're waiting for the new one: Gary.

He arrives, an artist with a slow, warm smile. Okay.

"And this is Grace."

Something is wrong here. I'm wrong.

Phoebe talks and talks in that breathless scattershot. Africa. Acid. Aging. All the A topics. I want to shoot her. The artist lists toward her like a shivering plant toward sunlight while Paul beats out some moody rhythm with a swizzle stick.

At last, Phoebe and Paul put me into a cab.

"He's not cute enough for Grace," I hear Phoebe tell Paul as the door slams shut.

Sometimes the married people invite you into their homes for dinner. They welcome you with tender, idiotic grins. They fold cloth napkins alongside your plate and drag down serving platters and pour salt into teensy dishes. Then they talk to each other, right through your eyes and over your head. We. We. We. You are appalled by the intimacy of their pronouns, the scary effort of their desserts. You imagine them collapsing against the walls in relief the second you're out the door.

Tonight Paul clears, silently Windexing every spot on the glass table, while Phoebe and I talk talk talk and four-year-old Lulu calls from her bed for more drinks of water. Finally, the table is clean and Lulu is quiet. We three settle onto the sofa, where Paul gives Phoebe a foot massage and Phoebe offers up a new blind date: Brad. A soap opera name. What kind of name is that?

"I don't know," I say.

"You risk being taken somewhere nice for dinner," Phoebe says.

"I think I need a lobotomy."

"I need a new pair of boots." We've been doing this since college. There's a quarrel buried inside it, a tiny baby seedlet, biding its time. About what?

But you have to eat.

This Brad person phones some nights later. I'm dining on Raisin Bran, watching *The Searchers* on TV. I wait patiently through all the commercials for the payoff. When John Wayne lifts Natalie Wood, his long-lost niece, into the air, I feel wonderfully sad. We make a date for the following Wednesday.

I live in a studio apartment on the third floor of a townhouse in the Village. Two of my windows front the street in an ordinary manner, but a third window is carved into the side of the house and offers an additional perspective. From this window I can see all the way down the street to Fifth Avenue. I see a sometimes-lover walking beside his wife. I see the sad bald ponds on the heads of briskly moving strangers. I see my UPS man unloading boxes of macaroni and cheese, the consolation prize I got when I appeared on *The $25,000 Pyramid* quiz show. I see a future ex-boyfriend hurrying away without his tie. What I am unable to see from my window is where the men come from before they reach my street from Fifth Avenue, where the men go when they reach Fifth Avenue from my street, and, most distressing, what becomes of the men when they choose to disappear in the direction of Sixth Avenue, which the limited perspective prevents me from seeing at all. As far as I know, the men cease to exist.

On Saturday afternoon, Phoebe and Lulu and I drive to my mother's house in Westchester. Phoebe is small but she drives like a linebacker. Once she's bullied the van onto the Bruckner Expressway she tells me what the problem is. "The problem is you don't know what it's like to be treated well by a man." Shame melts my earlobes. It's true, it's true. Paul shines her shoes and calls her Bunny. I've seen the notes in her *New York Times Cookbook: Paul likes. Paul doesn't like. Don't make again.* The next moment, I feel angry and insulted. Do I have to want what Phoebe wants? Can't I want what I want? What do I want?

The first blind date I ever had I never went on. It was a Friday night, freshman year at that second-rate college for girls we went to. It was snowing. He was a boy from a neighboring college—neighboring meaning a hundred miles or so. Perfectly dressed and doomed (my dating résumé had ominous, unexplainable gaps in it), I accepted the blind date from my official roommate, a girl with a hockey stick and cardigans. Then I fled to Phoebe-from-New-York's-room, to wait for him among her stacks of Pappagallo shoe boxes and the scent of Estée Lauder Youth Dew. Claire, who is dead now, and Nadia, a future lesbian, drifted in. We three draped ourselves across narrow, cluttered beds, smoked Newports, thumbed through *Glamour*'s breezy love advice. Phoebe stood before the vanity mirror in her pink terrycloth bathrobe expertly winding her frizzy hair onto fat rollers. Outside the flakes had thickened and were accumulating. Inwardly, I worried the question of boots–no boots as if my future happiness depended on the outcome. No one else had a date that night. My misery at the prospect of leaving this cozy female den was counterweighted by the tiniest balance-tipping grain of hope.

Eight o'clock came and went, and eight-thirty. Did I mention that the boy was hitchhiking? That he'd left word it would take him all day to get from his campus to ours? Phoebe had decided that she and Nadia would scout the lobby the moment the hostess buzzed the room to announce his arrival. At nine, when that rude sound interrupted Claire's reading of a one-paragraph letter from her high school obsession, everyone fell into their assigned rolls with guerrilla-like precision.

My attention slid away. I could feel the actual secret of dating reveal itself to me, no more complicated than the recipe for Jell-O. It was a romance—not with the date but with the untried self. Phoebe, born to be taken to dinner, was already a master of this exercise, but maybe I could learn. When Phoebe returned to the room at last, Nadia trailing behind, I was feeling genuine date anticipation. I was feeling good.

"You're not going," Phoebe said. Her face was a cheerful parody of bad news. "He's too awful. I'll tell him you're sick, or dead. I'll find him another date."

Her impressive authority, my shame and inexperience, the safe world of women versus the agonizingly unknown world of men, the weather, the footwear dilemma. Who knows? I released her—she marched off in that ratty bathrobe like a general—to deliver the news. It was a while before she returned. By then I was, in fact, feeling a little achy.

"What happened?" I asked her.

"He asked me if *I'd* go out with him." Indignant. That way she has of making a thing seem true and not true all at the same time.

"And you said . . . ?" asked Claire the literalist.

Phoebe tightened her terrycloth belt. You'd have thought it was mink. "I told him: I don't date."

"Do you want the mantel clock?" my mother says.

"No thanks."

"Take the side tables then. I won't need them."

"I don't think so. No."

"How about the linen place mats, Grace? With the matching napkins? Oh, and the porcelain dove centerpiece. Take it."

"No."

The house is sold, and my mother is moving to an apartment in the city. Phoebe and I walk through

the rooms to see if there's anything we want before the
tag sale. I'm not interested in my mother's furnishings.
Maybe the Ping-Pong table, in the basement. Ping-
Pong is my game. I could eat on it, too.

"I *love* this. Where's it from?" Phoebe says,
indicating a folkloric sculpture in the den—a man on a
horse. It's been sitting on that particular shelf for as long
as forever. I never really looked at it. I look at it now.

"From Guatemala," my mother says. "We bought it
in San Francisco."

"No, I'm taking that," I say.

It's a warm day in early June. The sun is strong
enough for bathing suits on the patio. My mother has
everything all set up out there. I've worn my suit under
shorts.

"Grace, have you read your horoscope in *Town and
Country*?" my mother says. "It's terrific this month." She
passes the magazine to me across Phoebe's knees. "You
know, you girls would love La Costa. You should go for
a week." My mother goes to this spa every year. She's
given up inviting me to come with her. Why would I
want to go to a spa? Even if I could afford to go on
my own, how could I possibly go without feeling as if
I were my mother? If I were to go, I could only go as
myself. It's hard to imagine.

"Sounds great," Phoebe says. "Let's all go. We'll get
massaged and exercised and toned up for summer. I'd
love a vacation right now."

Yvonne the housekeeper brings out three glasses
of iced tea on a tray.

"Where's that kid of mine?" Phoebe asks without turning.

"That little girl is in the kitchen with me," Yvonne calls out in her Jamaican lilt. "She's fine."

Phoebe is turning the pages of *Vogue,* her dress bunched up above her pale, freckled knees, blue heart-shaped sunglasses on her head.

"Phoebe, are you sure you won't change?" my mother says. "I have a black one-piece that would be perfect on you."

"I'm finished with suntans," Phoebe says. "They're unfashionable and bad for the skin."

"What one-piece?" I say.

"This issue of *Vogue* seems to be all about being gorgeous, not about clothes." Phoebe drops the magazine in mock disgust.

"So what do you think?" my mother says. "Am I too old to be in love?" Who's she asking? The green grass? The blue sky? Mr. Weigold fussing with his tomato plants next door?

"I'm too old *not* to be in love," Phoebe says. She doesn't mean to sound flip. "You're lucky," she tells my mother.

My mother is sixty, separated from husband number three, glamorous as a swan. Her lover is forty-four and married, not rich. My mother recently invited me to lunch in the city, to meet him. She wore a hat, rakishly tilted. The lover reminded me of my stepfather, the first one. Dark and handsome, with good hair, hurt eyes, a soft voice. Attentive, in a waiterly way. Nudging

30

the butter closer to my plate, passing the salt before I'd asked, helping me with my coat. His attentions caused me to feel a distinctly female disdain. I liked it. My mother had already explained that he slept in the basement of his own house because his wife was either too sick or too crazy to divorce. Still, my mother looked the way you're supposed to look when the person you love loves you back. Not agitated but serene.

"I'm panicked about aging," she says now with an apologetic laugh.

I look at her, her hair pulled back in a turban, her broad face streaked with Bain de Soleil, her shining un-made-up eyes. She looks exactly like herself.

Lulu's small figure appears on the other side of the glass patio doors. She slides them open with two-handed determination.

"Mom! Let's go. Now. Okay?" Lulu in a pink T-shirt and blue overalls. Her hair is colorless and thick, oddly brittle. It stands out from her head in spikelets, unintentionally punk. She won't let Phoebe's hairdresser touch it. He says she can never grow it long. I picture Lulu the teenager, hair down to her waist. Where will Phoebe and I be then?

"Not yet, baby," Phoebe says. "Tell Yvonne to get you some juice."

"Mom. I want to go now," Lulu says.

"We just got here, Lulu," Phoebe answers. "You're letting all the air-conditioning leak out. Finish playing Glamour Girls with Yvonne. Then we'll leave."

Lulu stands at the door, seeming to consider it.

"And then tonight I'm going to sleep in your bed, right?" the little girl calls out.

"Don't worry about the future, Lulu," Phoebe calls back.

There's nothing in my mother's house I want. Or else I want everything. Either way, I can't get rid of the longing.

When the sun slips behind a cloud, I take the tray with the empty glasses inside. The house has that good air conditioner hum. I don't see Yvonne or Lulu. I set down the tray on the empty counter next to the sink and peer at my reflection in the brushed chrome of the oven door. Then I take the back stairs two at a time and cross the upstairs hall to my mother's bedroom.

The thick rug, the bed big as the United States. In my mother's bathroom, I feel my usual pleasure in the deep vanity and double sinks. I open the medicine cabinet and shop my mother's makeup shelves, the stacks of shadows and blushers, the rows of lipsticks and thick bunches of colored pencils. I try a smudge of pink on my cheeks, smear something coppery on my eyelids. I swivel up lipstick after lipstick, each color worn to a pointy, cockeyed slant I'd recognize anywhere. Too familiar, like seeing my mother naked. I swivel each one down again. I check out the cabinet under the sink. There's a reserve stash of moisturizer and cleansing grains and astringent, directions in three languages on the sides of the unopened boxes. It even smells like a drugstore down here. I take one box of each, pack them into a striped cosmetic bag that looks practically unused. I'll take that, too.

"Do you live here?" Lulu is standing in the doorway, holding a brunette Glamour Girl.

"No, my mother does." I get to my feet and walk Lulu to a bedroom window. "Look." Phoebe and my mother below us. Phoebe's hand gesturing from her chaise. Something conspiratorial and easily female passing between them. Lulu turns away, unimpressed.

"Why don't you live here?" she says.

"Because I grew up and now I live in my own house. Want to smell good?" I choose a bottle from my mother's dresser. I spray my wrist and sniff. Then I spray both of Lulu's outstretched wrists. She sniffs one, then the other.

"Now my neck," she says. She cocks her head coquettishly and pushes back her hair. When I was seven, I dropped a handkerchief on Laurel Road hoping that bookish Walter French, trailing me home from school, would pick it up. Who knows where these things come from. Walter French ignored the handkerchief. By the time he asked me to the senior prom, I longed for some other boy disappearing just out of sight down our high school's long hallways.

I follow Lulu down the stairs. Phoebe is standing in the front hall, trying on one of my mother's big straw hats. My mother tilts the brim and leads Phoebe to an oval mirror. "Look at yourself!" she says. "You're gorgeous."

When Phoebe takes Lulu off to collect their things,

my mother says to me in a low voice, "Phoebe would like the dining room chairs. Are you sure you can't use them?"

"I really can't," I say.

Driving back to the city, I buckle up Lulu on my lap and hold her. Phoebe is talking about movies, about how she and her mother have never been to a movie together as adults. "It seems too dangerous, sitting there in the dark with my mother. What if something intimate happened on screen?" I picture Phoebe's mother, her large bosom and matronly suits, her long-dead only husband. Does not apply. I nuzzle the top of Lulu's blond head and try to remember the last time I went to the movies with my own mother. The scent of Chanel drifts up from Lulu's damp neck. I squeeze the little girl tight, breathing in the smell. "Hey, stop it!" she complains.

I have two kinds of men in my life. The ones I can talk about and the ones I can't. Lately I have so little to say I have to schedule emergency double sessions with Dr. Gold to get it all in. By the time I ride the subway all the way uptown to her office and emerge into the parallel universe of my psychotherapy neighborhood, past the tiny bank with no lines and the expensive strawberry store, I'm wondering what all the fuss is and how I'll fill all that time.

My married lover is a psychiatrist with a crumpled face who sees his own patients in an office exactly two townhouses down from mine. I feel related to him. An uncle? A cousin? The first time he climbed the stairs to my third-floor studio, we smoked cigarettes and paced the room nervously. "What are we going to do about this?" he said happily after we made love.

The next day, he called and said it again, this time anxiously. "What are we going to do about this?"

This is how it goes. His questions are parentheses I can curl up and live inside. Everything, I think. Or, nothing. I wonder what he thinks we are going to do about it, but I never remember to ask.

"What about his wife?" Phoebe said. "Don't you think about her?"

I try to think about her. Nothing comes up. "No," I say. I don't.

Some shopping virus overtakes me the day of the Brad date. I buy a frightening white cotton dress with big black splotches and bizarre sleeves. It's Japanese. The saleswoman has to stand on the other side of the door with complicated instructions about how to get into it. It's like learning Tampax. I buy other things, too. Pretty soon I've spent two thousand dollars. I'm amazed and appalled when the credit card goes through and everyone is still smiling. No one arrests me when I hit the street. I call Phoebe as soon as I get home and tell her what I've done. I'm still stunned. I don't have anything close to two thousand dollars. "Who do they think I think I am?" I ask her.

A few nights later, Brad is standing in my actual apartment. Exactly as Phoebe described him: presentable, in a navy blue blazer, which seems like a good sign, and an ascot, which does not. The conversation hasn't even gotten to movies and real estate and he's already talking about Phoebe, about the first time he met her. "She was standing in a doorway in a print dress holding the baby. She looked like a sexy Madonna." What is he, some kind of engineer?

Briskly, I gather up purse, keys, lipstick. "Ready?" I say. I feel like Miss Moneypenny. The Japanese dress is hanging in my closet with the punishing "Return for store credit only" slip stuffed into one of its bat sleeves. I've dressed for dinner in an intimate restaurant, in a simple, pretty neckline and earrings.

Out on the street the June air is delicious to breathe. By the time we reach Fifth Avenue, Brad and I have agreed that rents are lunatic and there are no good movies.

"Where are we going?" I say. I am a woman with a man. I can do this. At Fifth Avenue, we turn south.

"Chez moi," says Brad.

Oh no.

He lives a few blocks away, in a postwar apartment building with a sweep of circular drive and a doorman in shirtsleeves. There is a cooking odor in the elevator.

"To the right," he says, when the elevator doors open at six. As he digs into his pocket for keys, an image from prom night returns to me. Walter French's grim anxious face as he removed the orchid corsage from its box, his arms as skinny as they were in second grade hanging helplessly inside a dinner jacket as my mother deftly pinned the orchid to my dress. How humiliating,

I remember thinking, to have traveled all this way only to wind up back where I started.

"Here we are." Brad ushers me into a small, softly lit foyer. Just beyond it is a round table covered with a pale blue cloth and beautifully set for two, with candles and silver and creamy cloth napkins. I know I should feel flattered but instead I feel tricked. Who makes dinner for a blind date?

"I'll only be a few moments." He disappears into the kitchen, leaving me alone to read the bookshelves and peer at photographs. There's Brad, his arm around a small, dark-haired woman, both of them in shorts. A mountain looms in the background.

"It smells wonderful," I call out, studying the dark-haired woman.

"Sorry?" Brad reappears in a white chef's apron. He's holding a bottle of wine, dangling two wine glasses by their stems.

"Here, let me help," I say, taking the glasses from him. I follow him back into the kitchen for the corkscrew. Whatever's in the oven really does smell delicious. "You must think you live in a small town, leaving dinner to warm in the oven like this!" With its full spice shelf and worn wooden spoons, the kitchen has a cozy coupled look, or maybe it's the dark-haired woman in the photograph that makes it seem so.

"Well, I love to entertain."

Brad fills our glasses, and I carry them to the table. When we sit down to his first course, chilled shrimp with dill sauce, he tells me that he came to New York intending to go to film school and instead found himself working for a company that produces industrial films.

"We do some fairly innovative stuff. I mean, it's corporate sales and training, but some of it's pretty creative. And I get to travel—well, Phoenix and Atlanta basically—but it's really okay."

"That sounds good," I say. Film, film. I don't remember Phoebe saying anything about film.

Over the chicken with tarragon, Brad retells the story of the first time he met Phoebe. Nothing in his delivery suggests that he remembers telling me the story only an hour ago. He lingers thoughtfully over his description of the "golden, maternal light" she was standing in. What an idiot. My toes tap out a typing exercise I learned in ninth grade: *I could get some hot dogs for the team*. Brad serves the salad last, then espresso, serious and strong, in tiny white cups. My married lover and his wife have eaten at all the important restaurants in town; he grows arcane vegetables at their country house. They go there every weekend, every single weekend: two hours up, two hours back. He brings me ramps that he has grown himself. "Don't you think I'd rather be here, with you?" he says. What am I supposed to do with ramps?

By the time Brad brings out the buttery French pastries, all danger and possibility have long since leaked from the evening. I've begun to luxuriate in the arrogance of my own boredom. It's when I am dutifully writing down the name of the bakery and the maker of the beautifully designed espresso machine, mentally rehearsing my assurances that of course I can see myself home, and thank you again, that Brad mentions a name I recognize, and the evening rearranges itself into a different shape entirely. I realize that I've had this same blind date—this same blind date with Brad—before. It was the summer after college, when I was still living in my mother's house, commuting back and forth to my job in the city, at a magazine for teenage girls. I think it was the beauty editor's assistant who invited me to the beach on that sultry Sunday afternoon, along with her husband and his friend from school. I remember the heat, and my hair curling disastrously in the humidity, and the date's voice droning on and on about the films of Sergei Eisenstein, all through the hot afternoon and into dinner that same evening at a fish restaurant somewhere in Queens, itself a place more foreign to me than Russia, and how late it was by the time I got home, only to find my mother waiting up in one of her silky robes. I remember the expectant look on her face, so eager was she to hear every detail of the day and the date, and how her terrible hopefulness came at me like a wild pitch. By fall I had moved into Manhattan.

"It's incredible," I keep saying. I mean it.

Brad pretends to remember the day, and me, "in a vague sort of way," but clearly he isn't even a little bit tickled by the coincidence.

I'm more than tickled—I feel buoyed by the silly symmetry of these two wrong evenings. What I'm thinking is, I can't wait to get out of here, to tell Phoebe, and that carbonated feeling accompanies me into the spring night, onto the blocks of lower Fifth Avenue, and it stays with me even as I round the corner of my own street and look up to see the light burning in my empty third-floor window.

The next afternoon I am uptown in Dr. Gold's office, explaining my theory that this is one more specifically New York occurrence. "Like when you see a stranger on a Midtown bus first thing in the morning and then later that same day you notice the same stranger, but in some other part of the city entirely—in a restaurant or a movie line." I know that these things must happen everywhere, but that they happen at all in New York seems evidence of a design so inspired—well, you feel grateful just being part of the pattern. I tell Dr. Gold the word I've coined for the phenomenon: Manhappenstance.

Dr. Gold is silent. We just sit there. I struggle against the reproach I feel in the silence, and against whatever is behind the reproach, which is certainly worse.

By the time I've torn off my check for the session and taken the tiny antique elevator down to the street, I am picturing the stupid Japanese dress in my closet and my married lover spending the summer digging up ramps. I am thinking, you never find true love, you just keep reliving all your worst dates. What is wrong with me?

I stand there on the sidewalk in front of Dr. Gold's building and look west toward Fifth Avenue, where a slice of the Met anchors the view. A purple banner flaps in the sky above the steps, announcing the museum's exhibit: Pompeii A.D. 79. Normally I don't like visiting museums alone. I can't stop myself from thinking, Here I am, looking at paintings. But Pompeii is a disaster I've had a weakness for since high school Latin. And so instead of heading east in the direction of the subway, I make my way to the corner and cross Fifth Avenue. I sidestep buses and hot dog vendors and nannies gossiping over carriages, then pick my way up the steps, around the tourists and the mimes, to enter the tomblike cool.

In the central exhibit room I join a ragged line filing slowly past the glassed-in cases. There are coins in there and games and riotously colored mosaics, sculptured deities and earthenware bowls cartooned with pygmies in absurd erotic play. Rich people owned these objects once. One badly damaged fresco, said to be from the Villa of Mysteries, shows one woman with her hand cocked against her hip, the god Dionysus, another woman standing by, and a naked boy reading from a scroll. I squint at the tiny card that describes the fresco and learn that Roman women liked Dionysus best of all the gods. The fresco might describe a wedding or some other initiation rite, the card says, but no one knows for sure.

Ahead of me in line is a beautiful, black-haired young mother with a tiny child in her arms. I notice the way the young woman pauses in front of each display, then turns her head to address the child on her hip—the gesture alone suggests some private, perfectly enclosed world. Then I realize that the woman is

41

patiently explaining the contents of each case to the little girl, and her manner is so hushed and grave and exquisitely intimate that I can't take my eyes away. I'm embarrassed to be staring, but I can't stop.

The line snakes along, casually unravels and re-forms, and eventually the mother and daughter are lost to me. I move along with the crowd. At the end of the exhibit, just before the exit door, on a kind of landing, is the figure of a woman. She's lying on her side with her arms flung up across her face, hands clutching at the stony folds of skirt "to shield her" (the little card explains this) "from the black and choking smoke." She waited too long to flee, and the lava has preserved the shape of her distress forever.

Curvy

O*ne day I get tired of crying* and feeling sorry for myself—I'm not starving, I'm not in a war, I'm not crippled—and decide to track down my real father's phone number. Isn't it about time? I'm practically thirty-five years old. *This* is my life, right now. I call Cleveland Information. I don't know why I'm surprised when they give me the number. Irving Brandwein, as present and accountable as Macy's. I write it down on the corner of a takeout menu from Hunan Royal.

It's the Fourth of July weekend, a few weeks before Prince Charles is supposed to marry the shy kindergarten teacher. Everyone—meaning my ex-boyfriend and some crazy girl he broke my heart for—has left the city two by two. All that's left is me and my carefully chosen pile of new books (*The Complete*

Novels of Jane Austen Volume 1, The Interpretation of Dreams, Strangers on a Train), armature against the heavy air, the Sunday stillness every day, the whoosh of the occasional taxi, the Doobie Brothers coming from someone's open window. The soundtrack to the end of the world.

I don't know my father, not really. My mother divorced him when I was six, replaced him with a new father right away, then another one when that one turned out to be defective. The last time I saw him I was—what? Just out of college. He called to say that he was passing through New York for a sporting goods convention—that's his business, sporting goods or sports clothes or maybe sports trophies, something like that—and could he take me to dinner. Very polite. The time before that I was ten, when he took me to lunch and asked me why I wanted to change my name. This was in Cleveland, where we lived. My mother took the same care dressing me as I took dressing my dolls. For lunch with my father: patent leather Mary Janes and my brown tweed Chesterfield coat with the velvet collar. (The bowler hat with streamers felt babyish. I left it in the car.) I didn't have the heart to tell this almost stranger that Mother had changed our names, unofficially at least, the moment she remarried. "I just want my last name to be the same as my mother's last name," I said primly over chicken in a basket. My initial sense of importance—my brother, Alex, had been kept home at the last minute—was worn down by my father's soft, persistent questions with their alarming implications. I wanted to go home, to my biography of Abigail Adams and the new puppy our second father got us.

The last time my real father called, I was just out of college. Alex was still in school, in Boston. I asked if I could bring my best friend, Phoebe, along to dinner. Nothing that happened to me then was real unless it happened to Phoebe, too. My father was shorter than I remembered. Phoebe and I sat beside each other on the banquette, smoking and drinking gin and tonics, telling what we had studied at school and how we liked our first jobs, the two of us scrupulously avoiding each other's eyes for fear of collapsing into awful helpless laughter. The memory makes me cringe. "I'll wait for *you* to call the next time," my father told me kindly at the end of that evening. I guess it wasn't a great strategy on his part.

A few days later, I get up the nerve to dial the Cleveland number. She answers the phone. His wife. I ask for him, for Irv. That's how we refer to him, Alex and I. He's the original one-name celebrity. "It's Grace," I say. "His daughter." I feel like I'm calling the President.

"It's nice to hear your voice," my real father says when he gets on. His voice has the gentleness I remember, a little bit shy. He definitely sounds surprised. We say a few formal things back and forth but it doesn't matter what they are. It's like he's been waiting for the phone to ring. I know the feeling.

The next thing you know, Irv and his wife are going

to stop in New York for a day just to see us—me and my brother—on their way to a wedding in Florida. The first Saturday in August. They'll arrive in the afternoon and spend the night. So there's going to be a reunion: Me, Alex, Irv, and his wife. Not Mother.

"Have you told her yet?" my brother says. He has zero memories of Irv—he was only three when they divorced—but he's on board with the reunion. "Because you know she'll want to be in on it." Nope, I haven't. I've been relishing the secret. It's like walking around town with a concealed weapon.

"This has to be about *us*, not her," I say with big-sisterly authority. It occurs to me, though. Telling would be like actually using the weapon.

I say I'll explain it.

"Good luck," he says.

I take the subway to my mother's apartment on a Friday afternoon. We only have to stick around the office until noon in the summer. I work for a consulting firm that tracks novelty item and condiment trends. I write up reports for Howard and Josie, the two partners, put together focus groups, attend luncheons sponsored by Pez and the Pimento Council. Look, it's not the job I'm supposed to have. I can't even go into all the reasons I have it.

My mother and I sit on the terrace. She lives in an apartment house that takes up the whole block, but her apartment is on a low floor and you can see directly across the street into a firehouse that's been remade as a sculptor's studio. What an excellent New York view. I feel sorry for the sculptor, though. All he gets to look at is my mother's mammoth white brick building.

My mother has made iced tea for us to drink with the biscotti I picked up on the way. She's perfectly dressed, in pale linen afternoon clothes. She looks like she's just come from or is going somewhere. Where? She doesn't have a job, she doesn't see a therapist, she doesn't volunteer, and she has no hobbies. A mystery as usual.

"Grace, you know me. I only want this to be a good experience for you and your brother," my mother says after I've made my speech about who can participate in the reunion and who can't.

"Okay, well good." I sit up a little straighter. I like this feeling—gently but firmly forbidding my mother to suck up all the available attention.

We each sip our tea.

"Although I'd be curious to see Irv after all these years," she says. "That's natural, isn't it?"

Who knows what's natural? I ask people to share their feelings about tiny pickles. Is that natural?

"Have you discussed it with Dr. Gold?" my mother says.

"What do you mean?" She means, did you tell her before you told me.

"Does she think this is a good idea for you right now?"

"Why wouldn't it be a good idea?"

Recently my mother called Dr. Gold and asked her what she should be doing to help me. She and Alex

47

hover impatiently around my prickly unease like diners waiting for their table. "Be her mother," Dr. Gold says she told her. I wish I had thought of that.

Instead of going downtown to my empty apartment, I let my mother persuade me to walk around the corner to a neighborhood boutique she likes. My mother chats it up with the saleswoman while I peel off my T-shirt and jeans and try on a bunch of stuff in the dressing room. I come out in a strapless cotton dress with a matching jacket and consider myself in the mirror. I don't feel like me exactly, but do I feel like someone I might like to be? I try to picture my father seeing me for the first time in ten years. A sophisticated young woman. Nice shoulders, curly hair. Sexy. My mother runs her hand thoughtfully across the back of the dress with a small frown. I know that touch. It's code for stand up straight. I see what she sees: I'm crooked. One shoulder is higher than the other. I have no idea what happened to make my spine curve that much and no more. I don't even think about it. I'm tilted in a certain direction and that's that. I adjust my shoulder.

"I love that on you!" my mother says with a great big smile.

"And it's transitional," the saleswoman tells my mother.

I get the dress and some other stuff. My mother pays for everything while I pretend to be mesmerized by a scarf and jewelry display at the front of the store.

The next day I go to Bergdorf's for shoes. I tell

them to put it on my mother's charge. I sign her name on the slip and write "Daughter" in parentheses.

The following week, Dr. Gold and I start out with the upcoming reunion and how I feel about it and what my fantasies are of what might happen. I feel good, kind of excited. I have no particular fantasies. "I just want him to know what kind of person I've turned into," I say. But what kind of person is that?

I tell her about the shopping trip. Last winter Dr. Gold and I spent three sessions on whether or not I would accept a raccoon coat my mother no longer wore. Telling her about the new clothes is like confessing to some kind of junkie relapse. Just when I think I'm about to finally understand the nature of my bargain with my mother, a fog fills my skull and settles around my brain like a fairy-tale spell.

"That dress I got—it's not even my style," I tell Dr. Gold. I sound combative. Is the spell her fault?

"Well, how would you describe your style?" she says.

"Less, I don't know, *structured*. Looser. More flowy." I get a picture in my mind of Joni Mitchell, then Virginia Woolf, then Julie Christie in *Darling*. Folkloric hippie? Droopy thirties tea dresses? Mod London? A furious ball of misery and complaint has lodged itself in my throat. My eyes fill up. Why don't I have a style? Dr. Gold uncrosses and recrosses her legs. Now I worry that I've inadvertently insulted *her* style. Not that she has a style. When I started seeing her at the clinic two years ago, she wore jean skirts and sandals. "I'd prefer to see a man," I told the director of the clinic when he asked if I had a preference. "No particular reason." They gave me Dr. Gold. She was so new then she didn't get to go away in August. Now she wears silk blouses and tailored skirts and spends the entire month in Greece or Sardinia or Wellfleet. One of those places. It's almost a relief when people go away.

I find a room for Irv and his wife in a hotel on Park Avenue South. A good weekend rate and equidistant from my brother's apartment and from mine.

I call up my brother to tell him.

"I know that hotel. They shot a scene from *The Verdict* in the bar. Paul Newman slaps Charlotte Rampling across the face."

"So do you think I should take it?" I picture us all meeting in the dark woody bar after they've had a chance to unpack and get settled. I hear myself telling Irv and his wife that a Paul Newman movie was filmed here.

"Do whatever you want," my brother says. "This is all your idea."

I have a few memories of Irv as my father, that's all. I've combed through them with Dr. Gold: Irv giving me a stuffed monkey named Zippy, Irv hiding colored Easter eggs under the sofa cushions, Irv's pale calves sticking out of a bathrobe. Mother was the one who'd asked for the divorce. Why? Unclear. She's remarked that Irv could be "sarcastic," that he wasn't "ambitious," that he was "a little too short on the dance floor." She's said that it was a long time ago. Don't even try making someone remember something. It's like telling someone who to love. Irv remarried right away, too. My brother and I used to make fun of his new wife's name—Bettina. Wheatina, we called her. Peals of laughter. My mother laughed, too. We were big laughers.

"Who made that joke?" I ask my brother during one of our planning conversations.

"Probably I did," he says. "Why? What are you saying?"

"I'm just asking." Everyone is so touchy all of a sudden. Is there a law that says I have to find the same old jokes hilarious? This one happens to strike me as mean. And why does my brother still have all the basic facts wrong? He thinks Irv is from England.

"He's not?"

"He was *there*, during the war. But he's not *from* there. They were Polish Jews."

"Didn't he fly in that battle over Holland? The *A Bridge Too Far* battle?" We have a few photographs of Irv from World War II. There's one of him in his lieutenant's uniform. A bomber jacket and a cap. His face—his kind eyes, the shape of his mouth—is deeply familiar to me. "I thought Irv's mother was English or something," Alex says. He says it like he doesn't care one way or the other.

"I think she *lived* in England for a while. As a young woman." Actually, I'm hazy on the details myself. "Irv's parents—our grandparents—were socialists," I say. I feel proud of this.

"I wish I had that leather jacket," my brother says.

I imagine we'll eat at a nice bistro in the West Village the first night. Should I get theater tickets? No, it won't be that kind of visit. We're probably going to want to spend most of our time talking.

"If this is just going to be some superficial thing, if we're not going to talk about why he left, then I don't want to be part of it," my brother says on the phone one evening. I'm surprised by his sudden burst of feeling.

"What's he so angry about?" I ask Dr. Gold at our last session before her August break. "He thinks Irv *wanted* to leave. Where did he even get that idea?" I don't know why I feel so indignant. These are mostly rhetorical questions and Dr. Gold doesn't answer them. I talk some about work, about how the business is shaky and if it fails I'll probably have to go on unemployment and if that happens how will I even be able to see her because if I don't have a job where would I get the money? After that there's not that much to say. In the silence I can hear the clock ticking. The session is almost over. I wonder if we'll hug. When Dr. Gold asks me how I feel about her going away, I say, "You, you, you. It's all about you." It's not like I expect her to laugh. As far as I'm concerned she's already gone.

I met my ex-boyfriend—he's a writer who does freelance stuff for us—through James. James is our office manager.

"So what's his story?" I asked James after spotting this cute guy in the office one afternoon.

52

James is ten years older than I am, ugly and kind, with a large, pale head, doleful blue eyes, and thin hair the color of sand. The week I was hired, two years ago, a pipe burst in my office—we're on the third floor of an East Thirties brownstone—and I had to share with James for a month. We got to know each other. I learned that his marriage, to an attorney for the health and hospitals union, was faltering but that he didn't know whether he wanted to save it or leave it. Like me, he loved Fred and Ginger movies and old popular songs. He collected vintage postcards and tropical fish and rolled his eyes at the temperamental business practices of our bosses.

The game wasn't something James and I decided, exactly, just something we slipped into. We pretended that we worked for a company that made some nameless widgety product. We used our real names. But James was Mr. Appleton and I was Miss Hanford, the sexless boss and the spinster secretary. We were formal and repressed with each other, as if it were the fifties. When I moved back to my own office, Appleton Products stayed in business.

They're like small vacations for me, the game days. I completely forget to be afraid.

Other days, James wanders into my office mid afternoon, deposits himself in the chair opposite my desk, and tells me stories—about his mother who bakes pies and his father, a state trooper in Oregon. Or I tell him about my life, such as it is, and he tips back in his chair, hands resting on his belly, listening like there's nowhere else he'd rather be. I feel happy when I can make James smile his whale smile or shake silently with laughter. For minutes at a time I feel good.

"I don't know. Good writer. Kind of an asshole," James said.

He *was* good. I'd read some of his real writing, in one of the men's magazines. Sexy, too. Muscular and compact in tight black jeans, the sleeves on his denim work shirt turned back so you could see the dark hair above his wrist bones. Took me to a steak house on our first date. "You eat like a man," he said approvingly.

I sensed another woman in the background from the get-go. Well, in the foreground, too. An almondy shampoo was parked under his showerhead. A few items of clothing (cute, my size) were shoved to the back of his closet. His former wife. She worked for a United Nations agency whose name I couldn't keep straight in my mind. He said she'd left him for the Palestinian representative to Mozambique.

"Now what?" I asked Phoebe. We were watching television together over the phone.

"*Jeopardy!*"

"No. I mean, *now* what?"

"He's going to dump you five seconds after he recovers from his divorce," Phoebe said. "But wait—is he divorced?"

"Well, yes and no—I'm not exactly sure."

"Live dangerously. Ask."

Turned out he was, but only in the letter-of-the-law sense. He confessed that crazy girls held a fatal charm for him. The girlfriend between the ex-wife and me had been a shoplifter. "And how will you describe me?" I asked him once, pretending flirtation. "You?" He pulled me close and his hands wandered, sweetly tracing the shape of me. "You're not crazy," he whispered. "You're curvy." Curvy! Curvy has its charms, but crazy is love's Super Glue, the mousetrap that never lets go.

I'm the type who gets unhinged *after* love ends. What's saner than that? One night I rang his bell after midnight just to demand a more thorough explanation. "This isn't a police state, Grace!" he admonished. "It's just dating. Dating ends." It *felt* like a police state. "Don't you even have false pride?" he said, helping me off with my clothes. I said I didn't. Maybe I *was* crazy. "That's good," he said. "You only have real pride."

"Well, Miss Hanford, I'm glad to see you back at your desk," James said when I returned to work three days later, all cried out. "You're looking well. Your vacation must have agreed with you."

"Thank you, Mr. Appleton. Mother and I always enjoy our yearly week together," I said in my prim, pretend voice. That's another thing about crazy girls. They don't have mothers. They create themselves.

The day of the reunion I wake up with butterflies in my stomach. Their plane is supposed to get in at noon. My brother and I do the La Guardia–to–Manhattan arrival math a hundred times.

"He'll call me when they get into the room," I tell him again. "Then I'll call you. Then we'll meet them at the hotel. In the bar. Or you and I can meet outside and we can go in together."

I change clothes a bunch of times. In the end, I'm wearing the new suit.

When the phone rings I think I might be sick.

Alex is pacing back and forth on the sidewalk in front of the hotel, smoking a cigarette, when my taxi pulls up. His face wears a pained, distracted look.

"Are you okay?" I say.

"Stomach. I think I ate something bad last night."

The distracted look gathers itself, briefly, into acknowledgment of my costume. "Different look for you, no?"

I feign disinterest. "Father clothes," I say.

"Well, you look nice." He flicks the cigarette into the street. "Are you ready for this?" he says. My stomach flips.

The bar is pitch dark after the glare of the afternoon, but I see them right away, in a booth toward the back. They're on their feet the second they spot us. They look like tourists. Irv. Not too tall. Balding on top and puffy around the eyes. Kind of fit and muscular, though, in a polo shirt. Is that a cigar in his hand? I think I like it. Suddenly I'm remembering a bowling alley—pins crashing and the smell of beer.

Okay, here we go. Lots of hellos and handshakes and awkward embraces. I'm shocked by how *related* I feel to this man. The words form silently on my tongue: my father. Nice hug, and he's just my size, with a pleasing dryness to his voice and again, that familiarity.

Plus he's regarding me and Alex with so much, I don't know, pleasure, it seems he feels related to us, too. I feel proud of myself, like I've just given birth. Bettina is beaming.

"What would you like?" Irv says once we've arranged ourselves at the table, me and Alex on one side, Irv and Bettina on the other. No false heartiness in Irv's voice, thank God. A waiter approaches. Apparently, we all drink Bloody Marys.

But if not false heartiness—what?

Bettina fills in with, "You kids look exactly the same." I smile and nod, still speechless as a fool.

"It's wonderful, really wonderful, to see you both," Irv says then, like a meeting finally called to order.

"Awfully long overdue," I murmur. Am I at tea in an English novel?

Alex says, "Now I know who to thank for my receding hairline," and Irv smiles.

"Doesn't that come from the mother's side?" I say, but luckily no one pays attention.

There's a microsecond when the earth threatens to open and swallow us all (only Bettina survives), but in the nick of time I remember to tell the Paul Newman story—he's even from our hometown—and Irv looks around the bar again, impressed, retrieving from memory the exact scene in the movie, which, we all agree, was excellent. From there we slip easily into matters of historical review and record-keeping: Alex accounts for college in Boston, then the two years he spent in South America, running a small leather company. That's the official story, at least. I offer a funny anecdote about my job. I can do that.

"Did you know that your grandfather was an editor?" Irv asks me. No, I did not. "He edited the Yiddish newspaper in Cleveland." Hey. How about that.

Irv and Alex discuss the Red Sox' and Indians' pennant chances as if they're picking up an old conversation. Bettina turns to me. "Is there someone special in your life, honey?"

"No, not really, not right now," I say. I'm not interested in doing girl talk with Bettina. I'm listening to Irv and Alex, remembering how our second father took us to behind-the-fence dinners at the stadium. I'm reciting the names of the old players to myself— Woodie Held, Rocky Colavito, Jimmy Piersall—like it's some kind of poem. I'm studying the shape of Irv's eyes, hearing the music behind his words and his habit of punctuating his stories with fond, teasing banter directed toward his wife. I'm betting he tells war stories, the same ones again and again, and that everyone listens with real affection even though they've heard them all before. I'm thinking, he reminds me of someone, and then I'm realizing that it's me.

"His all-time favorite book is *Fear Strikes Out*," I say, indicating my brother.

After that everything quiets down. We all let it.

"You know, I wasn't completely sure I wanted to come here," Irv says. His hands levitate a few inches above the table, hover, then lower again.

My face wears an expression that says, Go on with that.

"I didn't know if I wanted to risk it. If it's not going to lead to anything more than this."

I nod. But I'm thinking: Lead? Lead to what? "I guess we have to start somewhere," I say. "Like, just to get some leverage." Whatever that means. The problem with spending most of your time inside books is you can produce words for any occasion. You just don't necessarily know what you're talking about.

"I have no real memories of you," Alex says abruptly. "I just know that you left. I didn't know why then and I don't really know why now."

It occurs to me that our second father might have put his fist through the wall in response to my brother's challenging tone of voice. That father had a temper. We neighborhood kids used to put on plays in the backyard every summer. I was always the lead and the second lead—princess, queen, fairy godmother. I'd deign to give my brother a minor role—dwarf, palace guard, woodsman. The summer we did *Sleeping Beauty* (I played the Queen and Sleeping Beauty) I happened to be kissing Kenny Baum, the King, behind our garage when Alex walked to the center of the lawn and delivered his one line: "There must be a path somewhere through this forest." Our next-door neighbor, Tommy Lantano, whose job was opening and closing the curtain, a blanket draped over the clothesline strung between our two garages, said, "Shut up, Alex," and I burst out laughing. Next thing you know Daddy has me by the arm and is hauling me into the house—for laughing or kissing, I'm still not sure.

"Well, the short answer is, that's the way your mother wanted it," Irv says. He says it in a resigned way, without a trace of anger.

"Are you sure you kids don't want something to eat?" Bettina says. Bettina isn't resigned.

My brother says he doesn't remember the day we were adopted by our second father, but I do. We're sitting on a hard wooden bench in the big empty hallway outside a judge's office. This would have been sometime after the day Irv took me to lunch. We're quiet, my brother and me, not even joking. I can feel my scratchy slip under my dress. Someone shows us into the judge's office. He's sitting behind a desk deep as a football field and piled with papers. (Was he wearing a black robe or have I added that?) We already know he's going to ask us which father we want. Even at ten, I know that this is only the pretend question. It's our mother we're being asked to choose.

The judge asks me first: Do I want our stepfather to be our real father from now on?

My mother isn't in that room with us, but my mother can see me no matter where I am. She can see all the way through me, everything good and everything bad. I've hidden my questions in a place so remote even I don't know how to find them.

Yes, I say.

Then it's my brother's turn. When the judge asks him, he says grumpily, "*Why* do we have to choose?"

"But you could have fought harder to be in our lives," Alex says now. "You never did." I stop breathing. I'm fourteen, waiting for Alex to jump off the garage one more time. When I watch my little brother act out this new ritual of his, it's like listening to Judy Garland sing "Over the Rainbow" on a record I have. You feel a little afraid listening to her, as if something terrible could happen and she won't make it to the end of the song. She does make it, though. She makes it every time. At the end of Judy's song, the audience goes crazy, shouting and applauding like mad. Someone yells, "I love you, Judy!" and she yells back, "I love you, too!" When Alex lands on the patchy grass, not on the asphalt driveway, I breathe out.

"Well, your mother made it pretty difficult," Irv says slowly as if it pains him to say it. "I'd take you out to dinner, and your mother would turn up in the same restaurant. Or I'd come to the house to pick you up for the weekend and she'd say that Alex couldn't come—he was being punished." I try to picture this: My mother and our second father lurking sitcom-style in plain sight. I can even see the challenging hat my mother is wearing. I glance at Alex, who looks frankly skeptical. "But I suppose the real reason is that I didn't think you two wanted me in your lives." Irv pauses. "I suppose I felt rejected."

I'm stirring the swizzle stick around in my Bloody Mary, poking at the piece of lime. He felt—what? Rejected? *He* felt that. By us?

"Well, we were just children," I hear myself say in my most queenly voice. "I mean, that's what we were."

61

My head is pounding with the wrongness of it. There's a whole new slant being introduced here. *We* rejected *him*. I'm not sure there's room in this reunion for that particular slant.

"It was a very big loss for your father," Bettina says. "It was a tragedy. He loved you kids very much." I understand something about Bettina suddenly: She hates my mother. The knowledge sends a thrill through me. I've never heard of anyone hating my mother. How *dare* she.

By the time the waiter comes around again we've agreed that the meet-and-greet part of the reunion is over.

My brother and I say goodbye to Irv and Bettina in the lobby, repeating the instructions about the dinner reservation and getting to the restaurant, then Alex and I make our way out to the street, tight-lipped, as if we're in danger of being overheard. It's overcast now, and humid, but the two of us stand at the curb, dazzled by the light, murmuring sounds at each other, the gist of which is, Do you believe this? Isn't it unbelievable? At fourteen, I didn't exactly know that Irv wouldn't be coming anymore, but he'd already disappeared around some corner in my mind. Judy Garland had replaced Anne Frank as the person I most wanted to be friends with. I imagined I might be Judy Garland's real daughter who she was forced to give to a family in Cleveland to raise for complicated show business reasons. I pictured the day that Judy and I would pass each other in New York City, walking down Fifth

Avenue. We'd exchange a look and know everything in each other's hearts without a word being said. The one thing wrong with this idea was Alex. He would have to be Judy's real son, too. Otherwise, how would we stay brother and sister?

A taxi pulls up, we quickly hug goodbye, and Alex opens the cab door for me. I get in, and he leans in toward me. I see the bright red poppy of my little brother's head, blood flowering through the blue cotton baseball jacket I made him pull up over the gash on the way to the hospital the last time he jumped off the garage.

"I wonder what he thinks of my hands and my elbows," he says now. "I wonder what he thinks of the scar above my eye."

It had been a few days before the Fourth of July, when my buzzer rang, startlingly, sometime after ten P.M.—a terrible sound. What had I done? James's voice came crackling over the intercom. Could he come up?

It was the first time James had set foot in my apartment—we didn't socialize outside work—and the fact of him standing there, his blurred, impassive face and mournful politeness among my things, my furniture and books and bed, made me shy and worried and, as a result, excessively flirtatious.

"It's you! I'm so happy it's you!" I said. He was looking around dismally now, soberly uncertain what he was doing there. "Should I get you a beer?"

He sighed, a complicated soliloquy, and ventured further in, and for a terrible moment I thought it was

Mr. Appleton standing there in my apartment, and for a more terrible moment I thought it wasn't.

"A beer would be welcome," he said. "I just thought I needed some, uh, exercise." With that he sank unhappily into the one easy chair.

"Ah." I nodded and hurried to the refrigerator.

We drank those, and then two more, me curled up in a corner of the sofa, James planted in the chair. As my air conditioner rattled and heaved, we talked about the usual things. He didn't mention what had propelled him out of his own home, and I thought it intrusive to ask. Finally, when he appeared ready to leave—he was standing, not steadily, and I was making thanks-for-coming noises—we wrapped our arms around each other and stood for a moment that way, my head against his chest, breathing together, swaying slightly. He smelled altogether alien through his damp T-shirt. Kissing him was frightening and necessary. The kissing carried us to bed, and once there our heads cleared. Too late, or possibly too soon. Either way, our sympathy for each other was unable to transform itself into anything we could get lost in. He left long before morning, pulling his clothes on like a hurried apology. This I sensed rather than saw. I was afraid to open my eyes.

"Take care, Grace," he said softly.

"*You* take care," I whispered.

My phone is ringing as I unlock the door to my apartment. It's Mother calling, wanting to know how it's going. "It's going good," I say.

"Honey, I'm so glad. I wanted this for the two of you."

Whatever it is she means, I feel a rush of guilt.

"Mom, I'm sorry about excluding you, but you understand, right?"

"Of course I do. In fact, I spoke to Irv just a little while ago. He invited me to join you for dinner, but I think not. Although he suggested brunch tomorrow."

"You called the hotel?"

"Just to say hello. Grace, I hope you're not angry. I couldn't help myself. I had to know what he thought about the two of you." I know that this is at least partly true. "I think he was happy to hear from me."

I picture Irv in the hotel room, sitting on the edge of the bed, talking to my mother. I see the half smile on his face as he lets my mother's warm voice wash over him. I see Bettina, stretched out next to him on top of the bedspread, her shoes kicked off, fuming. I know just how she feels. Still, my mother is the one I'm rooting for. That's just the way it is.

He's a nice man, my father. He's the nicest man my mother ever married. I know how the rest of the visit is going to play out. He'll talk about the past. He'll tell me things about my mother, things he doesn't mean to tell and that I don't really want to know, although somehow I already do. He'll confide in me, wanting to know what he can do to disarm my brother's anger and whether I think it can be disarmed. He'll want to know why I'm not married, and he'll inquire, delicately, if I think the divorce might have had anything to do with it. He'll want me to know that he's there for me, and he'll ask me to promise to stay in touch and let him know, really let him know, if I ever need anything. We *will* keep in touch. We'll exchange dutiful Sunday afternoon telephone calls and say "I love you" before we hang up. It's too late to have a real father, but maybe it's not too late to know I used to have one, once.

After the night with James, I spent several mopey days believing myself to be in love with him, several more certain I wasn't and was instead responsible for causing some serious harm. In the office, James appeared ambiguously jaunty, then stricken, treating me with an awful counterfeit casualness. Finally, I invited him out for a drink. "Why did you come over?" I asked him. It about killed me to do it.

He shook his head. "I like you so much, Grace."

"And now?"

"I'm married and you don't need that. God, it's the *last* thing you need."

I let his words, and then the kindness inside the words, seep into my blood and my bones. I said: "I hope I haven't behaved inappropriately with you, James, because I wouldn't want to do that, not with you—you, of all people . . . " I trailed off. That rickety little speech was the best I could do.

On Friday morning, the start of the Labor Day weekend, Howard and Josie summon James and me into the conference room and tell us that business is bad right now, and the firm can't support a staff. They have to let us go. I knew it was coming, I've known it for months. But now that it's happened I feel devastated. I start to cry. I cry and cry. How will I survive not being tucked into this little house with my family of co-workers? What will become of me?

James and I each have a cardboard box to pack up the stuff in our offices. Mine holds a few jars of cornichons and fancy mustards, some dumb novelty pens and retro Pez dispensers, but mostly coffee mugs and office supplies. When I look up, James is standing in my doorway. He's holding a white plastic crash helmet with the words "I saw Halley's Comet Coming" printed on it. It's his favorite novelty crash helmet. He clears his throat ostentatiously.

"Miss Hanford, on behalf of Appleton Products I'd like to take this opportunity to thank you for all your hard work and dedication," he says. He uses the bottom of his T-shirt to wipe off a thin layer of dust, then offers the helmet to me. "I hope you'll accept this small gift as a token of our appreciation."

It's the best gift anyone ever gave me—well, the most heartfelt. When I put it on my head I almost expect to hear the ocean. "Thank you, Mr. Appleton," I say. "No matter where I go in life, I will always remember my time here at Appleton Products." My words feel echoey as they bounce weirdly off the plastic, but I can tell that I'm saying what I mean.

While I finish packing up, I remember James telling

me something his father told him, about searching for people who are lost in the woods. The first thing the troopers want to know, he said, is whether the missing person is right- or left-handed. Apparently, people tend to get lost in the direction of their handedness. Everyone leans one way or the other. Someone who knows which way will always know how to find you.

The Secret of Drawing

*E*ven when *I'm packed up* and just about ready to leave for my first year of college, Alex is still asking, Did you call Daddy to say goodbye? Daddy isn't our real father, but he's been our father since I was six and Alex was three. My brother feels sorry for Daddy because he had to move to a crummy apartment out near the airport when Mother filed for divorce last year. Alex is the kind of brother who tears up right along with you at the end of *West Side Story*. I remember how Daddy's eyes looked the day he moved out, all red-rimmed. I still don't want to think about those eyes.

I meant to call, I did, but then it was the leaving day and I didn't. Alex and I wound up having one of our fights that morning—who knows about what—and when I was practically in the car and about to leave home for good, he shouted through the side door, "I hope you die! I hope you die in a car crash before you even get there!" Wham. He slammed the door shut. That's Alex, too.

"Don't pay any attention to him," Mother said. But when we backed out of the driveway, I could see him looking out from his bedroom window on the second floor.

Nothing's lonelier than your first night in a strange bed. My roommate, Betsy, brought her hockey stick to college. Just seeing it made me think I'll never find a friend. When Betsy turns out her light, I stay up to read the last pages of *An American Tragedy*. By the time I close that book, my original life is over. It's 1964. By the end of September I feel like I've been at Elmira College for Women forever.

"Allison Mackenzie cut off all her hair," Claire says one morning as I settle into my desk in eight o'clock English. Claire's inking a butterfly on the white skin of her inner arm.

"No!" I say. "She did?" I had to miss last night's show to write a paper for today.

"Okay, she didn't," Claire says just to be perverse. I like the way Claire smells. Like limes. She has long chestnut hair and the sweet round face of a pioneer girl. Who knows what goes on in Claire's head.

Allison Mackenzie is a character in *Peyton Place,* a television show Claire and Phoebe and I watch in the dorm lounge. It's based on a book I read in seventh grade, baby-sitting for the Bergers. I can still picture the book's black cloth binding and thrilling insides. Allison's blond hair goes to her waist, same as in the book.

Phoebe's clear blue eyes flick past Claire and connect with my brown ones. Recently, a boy I was slow-dancing with at a mixer told me I had sad eyes. I guess I'm the kind of girl boys like that like.

"I was the one who *told* that actress to cut her hair," Phoebe says. Phoebe's eyes are frank and challenging. Her hair is honey-colored, loopy waves tumbling to neat squared-off shoulders. She's small like me, but with bigger feet.

Phoebe draws hard on a Winston and tips her head back to blast the ceiling with her exhale. Phoebe is nervy, like my best friend from home. That girl is at the University of Wisconsin now. She sends me blue books filled with lavender-inked poetry and wild dating adventures in which she refers to herself as Scarlett. Claire's more like my second-best friend from home, the one who made Snow Queen Court and worried about her reputation. She goes to Mount Holyoke and dates a premed senior at Yale. Her stationery has the name of her dormitory at the top and a zillion exclamation points at the end of every other sentence. Those girls already feel as lost to me as Troy. I'm still the girl in the middle, though. I can go from good to bad and back again in a blink.

"I *wrote Peyton Place*," I say. "I *invented* Allison Mackenzie."

"You did?" says Claire.

"Claire," says Phoebe. "We're kidding."

"I know you are," Claire says crossly.

Phoebe reaches into her bookbag, fishes out a cigarette and tosses it to me. A big round box of powder rouge and a copy of *Miss Lonelyhearts* tumble out, too. The rouge rolls toward my desk. I stop it with my foot, then park the Winston behind my ear. When I bend down to pick up the makeup, I notice that Claire is wearing my Chinese slippers, the ones Mother sent from her trip to visit relatives in California. I try to remember the last time Claire was in my room.

"Cute shoes, Claire," I say. Her cheeks pink up, but she doesn't look my way.

I toss the rouge back to Phoebe. "I invented Blush-On," I say. Talking nonsense with Phoebe is fun, like the clapping game girls played when I was a kid. Hollywood. Clap, clap. Rhy-thm. Clap, clap.

"Cheez Whiz," Phoebe counters. "Also, by the way, the topless bikini."

"*Bye-Bye Birdie*," I say. "Book and music. Got the idea from Elvis Presley."

Phoebe exhales smoke through her nose in a snort of a laugh, then has a coughing fit. We're just learning how to smoke.

Claire is from Philadelphia, somewhere fancy, and has her original mother and father. Phoebe's from some part of New York City, and her father died when she was eight. Whenever I tell Claire and Phoebe a story with a reference to Daddy, Phoebe interrupts and says, "He's not your father, Grace. He's your *step*father." Well, I don't want to argue with her but the word feels wrong. My real father isn't dead. He's remarried, he lives in Ohio, and his name is Irv. Alex and I haven't seen him since we were small. It was always summer when he came, always around the Fourth of July, just before Alex's birthday. One year Irv brought us a puppy, a boxer we named Mugsy, and took Alex and me to a fancy restaurant we'd never been to. We ate South African lobster tails, right out of their bright red shells, dipping the meat into melted butter with special little forks. There were birthday sparklers on baked Alaska. Alex couldn't stop talking about lobster tails after that. He looked for them on the menu when we went to Chin's for chow mein, when we stopped along the road at Howard Johnson's. Those lobster tails must have gotten under Daddy's skin. After that, Alex got sent to his room when Irv came, and eventually Irv stopped coming. Mugsy chewed up the sofa cushions, and Daddy took him to a farm to live.

When Professor Thorne comes into the classroom in her strict wool suit and ironclad page boy, Phoebe mashes out her cigarette on her chair's underside. There's a commotion of sparks as the dying butt hits the floor, and my stomach goes hollow. Our assignment was to describe how a true thing happened. I didn't know what to write about so I wrote about something else.

"Let's get started," says Professor Thorne.

Claire's hand is in the air. "I'll go," she says, opening her notebook.

Claire's story is going to be about Bob, from high school. Bob Bob Bob Bob Bob. Bob's penis, Claire told us, is curved like a comma. Phoebe informed her that a penis can't curve. Phoebe and I agree there's something demented about the Claire-Bob thing—such as, does Bob even exist—but why hurt Claire's feelings? Phoebe has plenty of dates and is always expecting some boy to call. Me, I haven't had a boyfriend since Ricky Taylor in sixth grade when, boy-wise, I peaked. Don't bother asking me if Ricky Taylor's penis curves.

Professor Thorn calls on Nadia, and I breathe again.

Nadia begins. "I didn't know it at the time, but that Sunday would turn out to be the one Sunday I would never forget . . . "

If I look at Phoebe I'll burst out laughing, so I look out the window, at Mark Twain's actual writing room, which sits in the middle of our campus, at two long-haired girls hurrying past it through the drizzle. I look at the wet trees, at the leaves beginning to drop. One leaf, then another, then another after that.

I picked Elmira College for Women after seeing a picture of a leafy campus in a book on my guidance counselor's desk, then combining it in my mind with an illustration of a mail-order dress I saw while reading the cartoons in a magazine in my dermatologist's waiting room. I pictured myself doing a lot of reading at a place like that, probably under a tree. A girl's school seemed dignified, vaguely British. A college that a girl in a book might go to. A girl without the nerve to apply to a college anyone had actually heard of. Secretly? I have big plans for myself. Just don't ask me what they are.

Mother got cousin Larry to drive us there, because Ohio to New York was too far to drive alone, she said. I sat in the back seat and stared out the window. I concentrated on the yellow line down the middle of the highway, on keeping my edges crisp so my insides wouldn't leak out all over the back seat. Mother kept turning to tell me something new about a man she was dating. Percy this, Percy that. He lived in California, and wanted her to come out there for a visit.

"But do you approve of me going, Grace?" Mother asked. Her hair was still red, still in a bubble cut with cheek curls, the way Daddy used to do it. Daddy is a hairdresser and an orphan.

"Who's Percy?" Larry asked.

"You should just go," I said. I didn't approve or disapprove. Do you approve of the ocean? Do you disapprove of the sun?

While Mother and Larry chatted, I listened for "Pretty Woman" to come on the radio. Certain songs crawl directly into your heart. When Mother and Daddy came to visit me at sleepaway camp when I was eleven, I couldn't wait to sing "Old Shep" for them, about a dog that died. "Old Shep" is still the saddest song I've ever heard.

It was raining hard when Larry pulled up in front of a frightening-looking Gothic dormitory. Mother rummaged through her purse for lipstick. "It looks charming!" she said.

Orientation, freshman beanie, the meal pass system. When the welcoming assembly was almost over, Mother whispered, "Do you want me to go now, Gracie?" Some of the parents had already gone, and the rest were sitting on the edges of their seats like dinner guests who couldn't figure out how to leave. Mother sat beside me in her white coat and big sunglasses, a balled-up tissue in one hand. She looked like a bereaved movie star. When she took off the glasses, she looked like herself, only sorrier.

I didn't want her to go, or else I wanted to go with her.

"You might as well," I said.

That Nadia girl finishes up the story of her favorite uncle's heart attack. ". . . and looking at my uncle's pale face, I felt my own heart begin to break like the shattering notes of a single silver flute." Claire's arm is already in the air.

"Miss Silverman," Professor Thorne says instead.

Phoebe shrugs off her rain slicker—she's in her nightgown, a white flannel Lanz with little red flowers. Sitting there, back erect and bare legs crossed Indian-style—her muddy clogs are under her desk—she looks like a compact, cranky genie. She reads a story about the day a Pope came to Queens, New York, and passed by the Silvermans' apartment building on his way to Yankee Stadium. The band played "Hello, Dolly!" and even Rabbi Solomon's wife, watching from a balcony, fainted from excitement. Police officers were warned not to pray while on duty. You can tell Phoebe's story is true.

I think about my story, about the day my brother ran away from home. You can tell it's not.

"Do not mix work with pray," Phoebe reads in her matter-of-fact voice. She's a girl whose voice seems to say, Why feel sad? Why feel scared? Look around. The worst has already happened.

By the time I get called on, I've passed through my usual queasy terror and arrived at some still-under-construction new self. I stand. I pretend to read from my notebook. "You put your right foot in," I say in Phoebe's voice. "You put your right foot out."

I hear some nervous titters, then Claire's startled giggle, but it's Phoebe's big bark of a laugh I long for. "You put your right foot in. Then you shake it all about." I refuse to even look at Professor Thorne, at the pity I imagine in her eyes. Underneath I feel the way I always feel, terrified, and it's my job to pretend otherwise.

Then I hear Phoebe laugh, and I feel pretty okay. Not like me exactly, but giddy and light-headed, the way I felt the time cousin Rachel dared me to shoplift Go Go Go Pink lipstick from Woolworth's. "You do the Hokey-Pokey and you turn yourself around. That's what it's all about. Hey."

Mother writes every other day. She types her letters—she happens to be an excellent typist—on stationery from Exclusively Girls. That's the employment agency downtown where she's worked since Daddy moved out. Mother gets a big kick out of dressing up and going to an office every day, as long as it doesn't interfere with her new social life. When she went to California on the trip the slippers came from, this Percy person spotted Mother in a restaurant and practically fell in love with her on the spot. Now he comes all the way from Los Angeles, just to take her to tennis matches and the opera. Our family goes to the movies, then to Mawby's for hamburgers. Mother is always talking about the symphony orchestra and the art museum, but school took us there. I didn't know Cleveland had tennis matches. Mother says Percy used to date Dinah Shore. He's not a movie producer but he's got all kinds of ideas about how Mother could improve herself. Have her nose fixed is one way.

From the Desk of Georgia Hanford
Exclusively Girls
Employment Agency for Business Girls
Cleveland, Ohio

October 4, 1964

Dear Grace,

I'm writing to you on your 18th birthday, a day filled with many different emotions for me. You are entering into the adult world, a world filled with responsibilities and demands, etc. I can only remind you to reach out for all the goodness of life so that you never look back and regret that your youth was wasted on the young.

P.S. Percy flew in from Los Angeles again. He is that rare combination of charm, intelligence, glamour, humor, etc. We went to see *Traviata* (my black chiffon), then Chinese food after (he ate with chopsticks!). Next weekend is Al Abramowitz (Abramowitz Plumbing Supplies) and ice-skating and deli with Herb Cohen.

He wants me to come to Los Angeles, for opening night of the opera (formal, of course). I said I'd have to think it over carefully. Tell me, Grace. Do you think it's proper? I told him I couldn't do anything to damage the respect of my children.

I'm sorry about your laundry troubles! Will Claire replace the blouse?

All my love!
Mother

Alex sends a birthday card that really makes me laugh, and there's a dopey flowery one from Daddy. "To my Darling Daughter." At the bottom, he's written, *Please write!* and *P.S. I'd come and visit but I don't have the you-know-what.* A few words are misspelled, and I feel ashamed to see them. I shove the card into the bottom of my footlocker, along with the other cards Daddy has sent.

From the Desk of Georgia Hanford
Exclusively Girls
Employment Agency for Business Girls
Cleveland, Ohio

October 10

Hi Sweetie!

Just a quickie before I dash out to the dentist.
Grace, I do hope you'll reconsider the suitcase I sent
you. It's luxurious and elegant and you will be thrilled
to have it when you get married. Things at home are
relatively quiet. Alex and I had a run-in Sunday night
after you and I spoke. He is very definitely troubled
and wants discipline so badly. He keeps telling me I
have no control over him and I really feel this upsets
him. He asks, "What are you going to do about it?"
I don't have the answer. I can only hope for wisdom
and patience.

Love,
Mother

P.S. How was the Spanish Club tea? Did you or did
you not wear the hat?

College is one new experience after another. I have
so much to tell when I call home on Sunday evenings, I

can barely get it all in. The last week in October, Claire and Phoebe and I go to the airport with some other Elmira girls. We watch Bobby Kennedy stand on a car and tell the crowd why he'll make a great senator. We watch his hair flop onto his forehead. We watch him push it off. We scream and cheer, and a photographer for *Life* magazine takes our picture. Riding back on the bus, I imagine Daddy idly turning the pages of the magazine one slow afternoon, his feet up on a swivel chair, cigarette between his fingers, waiting for someone to dry, the way I've seen him hundreds of times in the beauty salon. I imagine his surprise when my face jumps out at him from the magazine. You wouldn't know it, but I'm wearing a fall. It's a fake length of sleek brown hair that makes my own wispy curls look thick and smooth. Everyone says it looks completely natural. Phoebe talked me into getting it. She taught me how to make my lips pale and my eyes more intriguing, too.

When our American Studies professor announces that the actual senator from New York will be coming to our campus next week, I think about going to hear his speech, too.

"You wouldn't vote for a Republican even if you could vote," Phoebe says when I mention it. "*Would* you?"

I feel a little bad for the man, that's all. It's the kind of bad I used to feel for a barrette I hadn't worn in a while.

"What if no one goes?" I say.

"You're too sensitive, Grace."

Phoebe Silverman isn't too sensitive. The other evening she camped outside the bathroom stall and explained to me exactly where the Tampax was supposed to go. It was a long explanation.

Later that night I told her the secret of drawing. I spend most of my time in Phoebe's room. Her real roommate practically lives in the library, then sneaks out to spend the night with her boyfriend. Sometimes I fall asleep in that missing girl's bed.

"When I was in the sixth grade, my mother went to Florida to visit my grandmother," I began. In my mind I could see Mother in their bedroom, see that single alarming suitcase of hers open on the unmade bed. Her late-night fight with Daddy still hung sourly in the morning air.

"Your grandmother who sends you coconut patties," said Phoebe. We've memorized the details of each other's lives, as if they're the combination to a lock.

The taxi beeped out front, and Daddy swung the suitcase off the bed. Alex had been dragging a balloon stick back and forth along the ribs of the radiator in their bedroom, and now he was stumbling around like a drunk, trying to balance the stick in the palm of one hand. "He looked like one of those plate twirlers on the *Ed Sullivan Show*," I told Phoebe. Daddy grabbed Alex by the arm and pushed him up against a wall. Mother went nuts, as usual. I spared Phoebe that part.

"God, I love those plate twirlers," she said.

I watched from the window as Daddy lifted Mother's suitcase into the trunk of the cab, and Mother disappeared into the back seat. Daddy shut the door after her, then leaned into the open window, his hands on the roof of the taxi, one foot propped behind the other. He said whatever he said, not that it helped. Then she was gone.

"One night that week, I was hanging out in my room, drawing," I told Phoebe. When I was a kid, I loved drawing horses. I could draw horses all day. I loved stories about pioneers, too, and when I drew I imagined a pioneer girl on a horse, galloping around a corral.

"Describe your room," Phoebe said. "Was there a canopy involved?"

She knew it was pink, but I said so again.

"My father came in." Shit. I waited for Phoebe to say, your *step*father.

"Your father who looks like a cross between Perry Como and Dean Martin," she said instead. Her voice was goofy-tired.

". . . and he stretched out next to me on my bed."

I couldn't see Phoebe in the almost-dark of the room, but I could sense her rearrange herself into a microscopically more attentive position. "What do you mean?" she said.

"I mean, he was lying there." I meant for her to concentrate on the story I was telling. "Then he took the sketch pad out of my hands. The pencil, too. He said, 'Watch. I want to show you something.'"

"Uh-huh."

Daddy has beautiful hands. According to Mother, his hands were the first thing she noticed. As I told

Phoebe the story, I pictured his hands, the clusters of black hair on each knuckle. "His hand moved up and down over the paper very delicately," I said. "The pencil barely grazed the paper. What he was drawing was circles. Sort of swirling circles that overlapped each other."

It was when he paused, then moved his hand away, that I saw an actual horse's flank, then galloping legs. I pushed at his hand to make him keep going. "Finally, he was done. He showed it to me. It was a perfect horse. He said, 'It's all circles. That's the secret of drawing.'" I still don't know where he learned such a good secret. In the orphanage where he grew up?

Phoebe was quiet, and I thought she didn't appreciate how truly incredible it was. Thinking it made me feel lost. Then I realized she was asleep.

Alone in the dark, I checked inside my mind for the dot. The dot's just that—a dot. It stands for Daddy and the way he used to touch me. Touch. Stop. Wait. I'd push at Daddy's hand to make him keep going: *More*. The last morning before Mother came home, he was in my bed. He was on top of me, sudden as a safe. I felt the surprise of air squeezed out between ribs, squashed heart thrashing. In the next instant, the weight was gone. The dot stands for the words he spoke next. "Oh, Gracie, this isn't good." Those awful words must have traveled an enormous distance because along the way they'd gathered the power to shatter the pleasure world into a sorry mess of shameful pieces. I was on one of those pieces, like that silent movie actress who floats away on a chunk of ice.

It was even lonelier when Mother came home. Everyone pretended I was the same Grace, when I was something else entirely. By now I'm used to the two Graces, one fitting just behind the other like a photograph slightly out of focus. And there's the dot. It reminds me there *was* a different Grace once. I look for that dot the way I used to look inside my jewelry box for the Snow White watch my real father gave me, or the way I looked for the plastic red feather pin from United Appeal I pinned to a bush when I was six. Mother and Daddy were away on their honeymoon, and Alex and I were staying with Uncle Sol and Aunt Ruth. I walked a different route to school each day and pinned the feather to the bush in case I couldn't find my way back. Just before I check inside my mind for the dot I feel the same dizzy uncertainty I felt when I looked for the watch and the feather. Will the dot still be there? And yes, it's there, it's always there.

Phoebe orders a pizza from Bruno's one weekend night when nothing much is going on, when no one has a blind date or a mixer or a paper to write. While we wait for the food, she reads us a quiz in *Glamour* that promises to match us with our ideal mate. "'Would you be happier on a ski slope or in a museum?'" she reads.

Claire is sitting on the roommate's bed, brushing her thick hair, flipping up the ends with long, mesmerizing strokes.

"'Would you rather spend the evening having dinner by candlelight or at a baseball game?'"

"Are we supposed to be writing this down?" Claire says, frowning.

"Would you rather slit your wrists or be a member of the Mitch Miller Singers?" Phoebe says. She snatches her hairbrush from Claire's hand.

We love magazines that promise to tell our futures, specifically who our soul mate is and where we'll meet him and what outfit we should be wearing when we do. Everyone says I'll meet mine in the library, and then they describe some shy bookish boy who worships me from afar. Some sensitive boy. I'm not saying my ideal mate shouldn't read books—just not all the time. I'd like to meet a boy who's really cute and funny and loves to dance and isn't counting on me to make all the conversation. If he were an existentialist or an atheist as well as a fraternity boy, that's fine with me. The thing is, I've read *Gone With the Wind* about a million times and I've never met a girl who wants to be Melanie.

I've got my art history book on my lap, and I'm highlighting the chapter on Etruscan art when reception buzzes to say the food's here. We three dig for change. We're always digging for change, for cigarettes and candy bars and long-distance phone calls whose charges can't be reversed. We complain about never having enough change, but we never talk about money. Grandpa left a few thousand dollars for my education when he died. That was a lot of money when I was two years old, but it only pays for about a year at Elmira now. Then what? When I said I was applying, Mother invited Uncle Sol over one night just before dinner to talk to me. He sat in the Early American writing desk chair that no one ever sat in. I sat on the sofa, my hands folded on my lap. I had never been alone in a room with my uncle before.

"Elmira is an expensive college," Uncle Sol told me. Mother worships her older brother. He looks like Yul Brynner, the King. He looks like he'd be the kind of father you'd be afraid of at first, then slowly learn to love, the way Anna learned to love the King of Siam. I was still learning.

I tried to think of the right thing to say but nothing came to mind. My cousin Rachel went to a state school, just like her brothers.

"Your mother doesn't have a lot of money, does she?"

"No," I said. Daddy didn't make much money as a hairdresser. When Alex was bar mitzvahed, Mother had to use Alex's gift money to pay for the party. Alex made her sign an IOU, but she still hadn't paid it back.

"It's pretty selfish, wouldn't you say, to apply to a private school that your mother can barely afford?"

I could hear Mother in the kitchen, rummaging in the silverware drawer. My cheeks blazed with shame. I wasn't great, but I was better than Rachel.

Uncle Sol stood and looked down at me. His hands were on his hips, just like the King. "Enough said?"

That was it. I was definitely going.

Phoebe goes to get the pizza while Claire creams her hands with something she's picked up from the missing roommate's vanity. I notice for the first time that Claire is wearing my charm bracelet, the one Daddy bought me for Sweet Sixteen.

"Even though you don't talk about sex I think you like it," Claire says out of the blue. Funny, it feels like a compliment.

"Oh, Claire," I say.

When Phoebe returns with the food, we open the big box, and the steamy smell of tomato sauce and cardboard washes over us. We tear into the food, the way we always do. You can say one thing for us. We're never not famished.

"Remember: This is a race," Phoebe says.

As soon as November arrives, the air turns raw, and the idea of home begins to re-form in our imaginations. Thanksgiving is just ahead, past the presidential election we've been talking about in American Studies, past midterm exams, past the last of the fall mixers with the boys who populate the schools around us.

Mother mentions Percy, the man from California, in every letter. I know that Percy smokes a pipe and wears tweed jackets with leather elbow patches, and Mother makes a point of telling me he's "well-read." Mother's vivacious and nice, but she's impressionable.

Phoebe and Claire get a big kick out of her social life, and I've taken to reading some of her letters out loud. "I am sure I love Percy," Mother wrote in the last one, "but I keep reminding myself that I loved Al, too, at one time, and Herb." I look up—they're hanging on every word. "Percy is like no one in the world I have ever known," I continue. "I trust him so completely with all our lives. He weaves words into the most beautiful patterns. He talks from his heart and soul." Claire claps her hand over her mouth. Phoebe snorts admiringly. When I read Mother's letters out loud, I know who I am. I'm the girl with the dating mother.

Claire and I wind up going to the senator's speech together. He's old and elegant and kind of boring and his hair doesn't flop. I can barely keep my eyes open, and Claire keeps pinching me to stay awake. When the speech is over, we don't hang around with the pale, serious girls to shake his hand. What's the point?

"Well, it's his own fault," Claire says apropos of nothing.

I don't know why this makes me laugh. "He has no one to blame but himself," I say.

We walk over to the dining hall to get in line for supper, and we keep saying stuff like this back and forth and over and over, just nonsense, so many times and with so much feeling we forget what we mean, but each time we say them we laugh harder and somehow they feel truer. The thing is, Phoebe is clever and brave, but Claire has this sly sense of humor that sneaks up on you if you let it. I feel protective of Claire. I'm never sure she's even playing the same game.

The bulletin board outside the dining hall is already papered over with requests for rides, with ads for airline and bus tickets. At the table, as we pass the platters of food around, the names of friends from home are resurfacing in the hum. Tonight, for example, Claire announces receiving a few Bob sightings from one of her hometown friends. Bob at the high school track field. Bob at a bar in a distant suburb. Bob's car parked in front of Quality Cleaners.

"Are you going to see Bob when you're home?" Phoebe asks her.

"Oh. Well, I guess so," Claire says, as if the idea is only just occurring to her. She draws out the word *guess*. She adds, "He called last night around three in the morning— drunk. He wanted to drive here, from Philadelphia. I had to make him swear not to get into a car."

It's impossible to know if this is true. Claire has a single room, for one thing. No one knows how she got it.

Phoebe's made a zillion plans with various boys for over Thanksgiving vacation. It's weeks away and she's already booked.

I'm not booked. I have a letter from Mother saying Percy will be "joining us." This letter I read to myself, even though it's filled with details about Mother's trip to Los Angeles, with little drawings of the outfits she wore to each event. She reminds me to make airline reservations and asks me to please remember to send Percy "a nice note." A note about what? I turn the words "joining us" over and over in my mind, and each time I do they feel more pretentious.

Still, we're all excited, including me. We can't wait for our triumphant return. We want to show off our new superior college selves. We're practically giddy with anticipation. The dumbest things make us laugh. "This is only going to end in tears," Phoebe takes to saying in a fake-parent voice, and this causes us to laugh even harder, until our cheeks are wet, until we have to clutch our stomachs and beg each other to please stop.

If Phoebe or Claire or I feel uneasy at the thought of leaving each other for those other places, no one mentions it. We act as if we're not secretly jealous to be reminded of each other's former best and closest friends, the former best and favorite pizza parlors and shopping centers and movie theaters and record stores, the former lives whose landmarks we thrilled to turn away from two brief months ago—but a lifetime is what it feels like now. We talk the way we always do. We plan what we'll do in the weeks and months after Thanksgiving, after Christmas, after freshman year, after graduation: drive to New York, fly to Florida, travel around Europe, lose our virginity, get an apartment together, fall in love, be bridesmaids in each other's weddings. We talk the way we always talk, in code, in sly asides, in puzzles and jokes, as if saying plainly what's in our hearts could cause us to burst into flames.

One morning, a note is slipped under the door of my room, saying there's a Special Delivery letter for me in the campus post office. I hurry over before breakfast. The small building is empty of students, but there's an attractive dark-haired woman in a suit, a silk scarf knotted at her neck. She's busy cutting open several small cartons clustered on the floor around her.

I peer into my mailbox and find a single envelope. It's business-sized, thin as a rejection. Due to the purple date and time stamp and the long row of stamps, though, to the words Special Delivery and Air Mail underlined three times beneath my name and the name of my dormitory, all those typed in big black capital letters, the flimsy envelope feels swollen with self-importance. It's from Percy Perry.

My dearest Grace:

I am so looking forward to meeting you as well. I'm very, very impressed with you and your scholastic achievement. It's wonderful to know that in addition to being so sweet and pretty, with such winning charm, that you're also blessed with brains! What a catch you'll make for some lucky boy! Don't ever sell yourself short, my dear Grace. And if you're ever feeling low and depressed, or things don't work out just right—either in school or socially—drop me a line or call, and I'll try to cheer you up. Remember, you have a sincere and devoted friend in me, to whom you can turn for emotional, spiritual, and mental nourishment at any time. You're always in our hearts, and in mine with particular emphasis and warmth, because I've never had a daughter before!

All my love,
Percy

I put it right back into its flimsy envelope, swollen myself with some wrong combination of embarrassment and pleasure. So these are the words he weaves around Mother.

The woman is speaking to me. I look up, as if I've been caught reading someone else's mail. I see that she's torn open the cartons and is unlocking one long swinging wall of mailboxes.

"Are you free for an hour or so?" she says. She offers me a warm, inviting smile. I smile back. I see now that the cartons are filled with books, all the same book, one with a soft red cover and bold black type

I slip Percy's letter into my Spanish book.

It takes us under an hour to put one book into each mailbox, and though my back feels achy when we finish, I am twenty dollars richer. I don't ask why each girl is getting a book written by Barry Goldwater, the Republican candidate for President, and I don't particularly wonder. I feel virtuous for having done a job and earned twenty dollars. I feel absolved of something I can't name.

By the time I return to the dorm late that afternoon, everyone who's picked up mail has one of the books, even if they haven't read it. Phoebe has read it. I've never seen her so mad. Her outrage has infected the dorm and is beginning to spread over the campus. She's turned into a small general marshaling troops. "Propaganda," Phoebe calls it. "Political scare-mongering." By dinner she's organized a candlelight march to protest what she calls "the school's passive tolerance for the distribution of propaganda."

I don't say a word about my role in distributing

the books. I'm not entirely sure what, if anything, I've done to contribute to this injustice, which I admit I understand only vaguely. It takes me by surprise, my ignorance of the world. It startles me every time.

That evening, I make myself invisible. I join the long line of candlelit girls, some wearing their class blazer, in the procession that crosses campus, weaves around the pond, and makes its way to the president's house. We girls are muted and polite, careful not to tread through the flower beds as we gather in front with our flickering candles and nicely lettered signs, and though our mostly well-behaved discontent is punctuated by a few rude shouts, we return to our dorms in an orderly fashion well before curfew.

It's not until the next morning that we realize Claire is gone.

In Thorne's class, someone mentions a car coming for her last night—right after supper, someone else says.

Was it Bob? No one can say for sure. That Phoebe! So busy getting everyone riled up about the books, we didn't notice Claire was gone.

After class, though, Phoebe and I go together to the assistant dean's office. Claire's mother came for her, the woman in the administration office tells us kindly. Claire has transferred to a school in Pennsylvania, it seems. We're dumbfounded, but it's possible. Parents have that kind of supernatural power. And after all, it's Claire.

But the notecard that turns up in my mailbox a

few days later isn't from a college in Pennsylvania. It's from a psychiatric hospital in Maryland.

Dear Grace and Phoebe,

I'm sorry I didn't get to say goodbye! Pls. save me some pizza and, if you get a chance, forward my good leather gloves (in an orange box, possibly under my bed) to this address. I love you! Claire

Phoebe and I forget about classes. We get the phone number of the hospital from Information and call it the second we get back to the dorm. We call person-to-person for Claire. And when the operator returns to say that Claire is unavailable, we scrounge up a pile of change and dial the number direct. Tell her to call this number, we say in an urgent voice to whoever has answered the phone. Tell her to reverse the charges. We spend the rest of the day in Phoebe's room, in case Claire does call. I'm not mad at Phoebe anymore. She's as upset about Claire as I am. We keep the door half open, listening for the phone down the hall. While we wait, we tell Claire stories. Claire on her hands and knees in Early Childhood Development hunting for her lost false eyelash. Claire mimicking the way the salesman at the Gorton Coy department store mispronounces *chic*. Claire's dirty feet. We debate the existence of Bob and wonder if Claire has been taken away to have an abortion or whatever is worse.

I haven't told Phoebe my news. Mother and Percy are going to be married. At Christmas. We're moving to California right after the first of the year. Alex is excited, Mother said during Sunday's call, because he's going to have his own car. And Percy definitely thinks I should apply to a college in California for sophomore year. Mother says Percy has a friend who's going to arrange a private tour of a movie studio for us when I fly out for the first time, on spring break. I guess we've been saved, and at the very last minute.

Claire doesn't call. But even when the sky has darkened, Phoebe and I are still listening for the ring. Phoebe has crawled under her covers in her nightgown. I've tucked the roommate's quilt over my wrinkled skirt. When it's clear we've missed the second dinner seating, we're still listening. We owe Claire that much, don't we? We sing "Cathy's Clown," trying to get the harmony right between the two beds. Phoebe tells the story of color war at Camp Winihawk, and I recite the three things I know by heart: An Emily Dickinson poem called "I Died for Beauty," the Gettysburg Address, and the Crest toothpaste slogan. At eight-thirty, it could be three in the morning. Phoebe and I are quiet, not even smoking, and the room is dark except for the little lights around one of the vanity mirrors. I lie on my back and twirl the flippy ends of my fake hair. I watch as shadows form and re-form on the ceiling whenever a girl passes the room on her way to the kitchenette. The shadows begin to resemble waves, and the room, we two girls tucked inside it, feels safely adrift on currents of silence and talk.

At the sound of a rap on the door we startle. It's my roommate, Betsy. She pushes the door open wider but keeps her body planted on the exact other side of the threshold. What a disappointment I am as a roommate. "Your father is here to see you," Betsy says sternly.

For a moment, I picture my real father, the one who's been scissored out of all the old photographs. In one of them, his disembodied right hand—there's a chunky ring on one finger—rests on a nightclub table crowded with filled ashtrays and lipsticked glasses. Uncle Sol and Aunt Ruth are at the table, and Mother, with Rita Hayworth hair and a cigarette holder. Mother's eyes wear a dreamy expression, as if she's already picturing something better.

Phoebe snaps on a light. "I'll come with you, Grace," she says. She's out of bed, pulling on clothes.

"Don't be silly," I say, scrunching my eyes against the sudden light. What's the emergency? I get to my feet. I smooth my skirt and check the mirror to make sure my fake hair's on right.

I follow Betsy down the hall, and when she peels off in the direction of our room, I continue down a flight of stairs to reception.

Daddy is standing beside the resident advisor's desk. The same thick black hair, glistening now with rain. The same bruised eyes and stormy mouth.

"Daddy." My mouth is stale. I feel kind of dazed.

"Hi, sweetheart." He opens his arms. I walk up to them but not into them. I kiss his rough cheek like I'm dispensing a chilly favor.

LESLEY DORMEN

"You didn't tell me you were coming," I say in my Snow Queen voice. Or did he? I think guiltily of all the cards I've stuffed into my footlocker.

"Well, I missed you."

"Oh." My real voice sounds tiny.

"Show me around, why don't you? Let me take you to dinner."

"Men aren't allowed in the rooms," I say. I'm panicky at the thought of Phoebe seeing him. I don't know why. "Wait here," I tell him. "I'll go get my coat."

Just like that, we walk out into the damp night. I feel like a lump of snarling deadweight, like I've been collected by one of those blind dates you can't help but despise for not recognizing from the very first second that there's no future in it, that the whole evening will be a seething, tiresome charade. Daddy opens the passenger door of the car for me, and I slide in, modestly hurrying my knees back together, tugging my A-line skirt down to cover them.

It smells like car in there, like leather and smoke. It smells like driving downtown to a Technicolor movie, like the long trip to Washington, D.C., to see the cherry blossoms. It smells like child time, like the endless present tense of family.

Daddy walks around to the driver's side and gets in, and as he puts the key in the ignition, and the motor turns over, I'm a Brownie on her way to father-daughter potluck. I push in the cigarette lighter and flick on the radio, and a deeper ribbon of memory is released—the cozy sound of a baseball game coming over the car radio, cigar smoke, an unnamed ocean of feeling so blissful and radiant it makes my heart hurt. Joy. The lighter pops out. The ribbon is gone. I fish a Newport from my purse.

"You smoke," Daddy says. Like I went bad after all.

"Everyone smokes." I turn away and huff my steamy breath onto the side window, then watch my ghostly mouth melt away. It startles me to see my own reflection flash briefly back at me in the window glass, my sulky eyes and glamorous hair.

We drive to the Tom Sawyer Diner, a place I'm pretty sure no one goes. It's the cheapest nice-enough restaurant I can think of.

I slide into one side of a booth by the window. Daddy hangs his wet jacket on the coat rack, then slips in opposite, removing the pack of Kents from his shirt pocket, the heavy silver lighter from his pants pocket. He lays these things on the table like he's just been arrested. I shrug off my coat, start paging through songs on the miniature table jukebox.

The waitress brings menus. "A Coke for my daughter," Daddy tells her in his deep, flirtatious voice, as if he's answering a question he alone can read on her pretty young face, and all for my benefit.

I don't even look at him. I hunt for loose quarters in the lint and tobacco at the bottom of my purse. I feed quarters into the jukebox, punch in numbers for songs.

"Your hair's gotten long," Daddy says.

"It's a *fall*," I say as if anyone with a brain could see that.

"I hear your mother put the house up for sale." Daddy lights up a Kent, takes a drag, holds it like a pencil, eyes narrowing against the smoke.

"Yeah."

We order whatever we order, and the food comes, and we busy ourselves over it for a while. I wait like a frozen girl for each song to come on, and when it does, I hurl myself inside like it's a lifeboat. Daddy says he has a second job, driving a cab nights. He says, "I'll be able to send you spending money, sweetheart." It practically makes me cry, it's so pathetic.

I can hear Alex say, "That'll be the day." He says it just like John Wayne, in *The Searchers*. "That'll be the day." Alex and I love that movie. We can't see it enough times.

Daddy says he still goes to the orphanage once a month to cut the little girls' hair for free.

"Uh-huh," I say. I immediately picture the pale yellow brick of that place, even though I went with Daddy one time only. I waited for him in the car. Orphans terrified and fascinated me. Afterward, in my room at home, I thought about the unfortunate sad-eyed girl probably my same age who I imagined lived there, the girl whose bangs Daddy trimmed because, he said, he knew what it was like to grow up in a place like that. She was the girl I imagined when I drew the horse.

"Thank you for dinner," I say politely when the waitress has dropped the check on the table and

100

Daddy is fishing out his wallet. He smiles, looks sort of surprised and pleased. Doesn't even know a lie when he hears one.

It's quiet on the way back. I don't bother with the radio, just stare out the window. We're driving, and everything is what it is. What it is is the opposite of *The Wizard of Oz*. That movie switches from black and white to color as soon as Dorothy gets to Oz. My life started out in color, then it switched to black and white. When we pull up outside the dorm, I feel like I could sleep for a week.

I'm not big on goodbyes. I don't like saying good night if I can help it. I lean over and kiss Daddy's cheek anyway. "Drive carefully, Daddy," I say as I get out. But the words come out ragged. I wonder if I'll never see him again.

I don't go in right away. I stand there after the car's pulled away. I shift from foot to foot, blinking back tears and hugging myself against the cold. I watch until I can't see that car anymore, until all that's left is a howl the size of a dot.

I Asked My Mother

I called my mother and asked her if I could have two thousand dollars.

She said I'd have to wait until after her face-lift.

I said I needed it now.

She said, "You're not critical of me for getting a face-lift, are you?"

"Of course not," I said. "I hope you'll give me the money when I need mine."

My mother was eating Lean Cuisine in her dining room and I was eating pork lo mein on my bed. We were in the same time zone but at a distance.

"I'll call you back," I said. "I have another call."

It was my married lover, from a pay phone. I hurried out to meet him in the kind of restaurant that has Christmas decorations year-round. It went well.

After we parted I went to an expensive store and bought a wardrobe for our future life together: resort clothes, city clothes, hostess skirts.

"Enjoy them!" the saleswoman said.

"I know I will!" I said.

I dragged the shopping bag behind me like a crabby, overtired child.

When I got home I added up the column of numbers in my checkbook. Then I called my mother back.

"I made a mistake," I told her. "I need four thousand dollars. And I need it next week, at the latest."

My mother said things were different now because her husband was bankrupt. "There isn't any money," is how she put it.

She said she'd try to come up with something while she was at the spa. She told me she wasn't flying first-class. "Those days are over," she said.

I put my mother on hold to take another call. When I came back, we talked about other things. I asked my mother if she had any clothes I could have.

"There's a suede jacket," she said. "I've had it for fifteen years. It's never even been dry-cleaned." She said I couldn't have the fox coat.

I was feeling warmly toward my mother. I told her I might come to visit her soon. "But I'm not promising," I said.

I called my mother and asked her if she wanted lunch or dinner on her birthday.

She said, "If we have dinner, what will I do with the whole day?"

I wanted to know why my mother felt entitled to a whole day but I changed the subject. I told my mother I had a new haircut I liked.

"Is it short?" she said in an excited voice. "I love your hair short!"

I told her it wasn't short. "I hate my hair short," is what I said. I hadn't intended to change the subject that much.

I was on the phone in my apartment and my mother was on the phone in hers. It was bright and warm outside, it was afternoon, it was Sunday—the worst possible combination of features.

"Did you see *Dynasty* the other night?" my mother said. She was eating coffee-flavored Nips, two at a time. I could hear them.

I pretended I had never heard of such a program and was insulted to be asked about it. I didn't say I was watching *Little House on the Prairie*.

"What are your plans?" my mother said.

I heard a noise in the hallway outside my door. I tiptoed to the door with the phone cradled to my chest. I looked through the peephole. No one was there.

I asked my mother, "What am I going to do?"

My mother asked me what I meant.

I looked around at the objects in my apartment: A fake ficus tree, some posters tacked to the walls, the complete works of Anita Brookner. Each object seemed to possess enough ill will to bludgeon me senseless.

I said the same words again.

Because of the Nips I couldn't tell if my mother said, "This is your year to be married" or "You could get a job as a receptionist."

I flipped through my address book to see who else to call. There were the people in the present. There were the people in the past. There were the people with too many crossed-out and rewritten area codes. There were the jury duty and the tap-dancing class people it had been a mistake to use ink on. All the rest were the people it was impossible to call.

When I hung up, I opened the door and stuck my head into the hall. I looked around but no one was there. From inside my apartment I could hear the phone not ringing. I could hear the people I couldn't call not calling me.

I called my mother to ask her to call me and leave a message. I needed to know if my answering machine was working.

Her answering machine answered. I hung up before the beep.

Then I immediately redialed her number. She picked up.

"Where were you!" I demanded. I didn't really want to know, I was just being polite.

"I need to have a serious talk with you," my mother said in a stern voice.

I took the phone away from my ear and made a gagging face at it. I interviewed the contents of my refrigerator. I looked out the window to see if my lover might be passing by with his wife. I examined my pores in a magnifying mirror. I waited for the part where my mother said, "I have to be able to say what I feel, don't I?"

"Can you call me back?" I said.

When the phone rang again, I let my answering machine pick up. After the beep, my mother said in a bright, flirtatious voice, "Testing! Testing! Hello? This is your mother calling!" I threw myself across my bed and wept.

The phone rang and rang and rang. I dared myself to believe it could be anyone.

"I just want you to have what you need," my mother said after the beep.

I've dared myself to play that old tape once or twice. "I just want you to have what you need," my mother says now and for eternity after the beep. The voice sounds just like my mother's voice, and that's how I know the words are true.

I called the floor nurse and asked her if my mother was conscious.

She said she was the same.

I hovered over my mother's bed.

"Mom?" I said. "Mom?"

My mother didn't answer.

I sat in the window. I stared at the park.

I hovered over my mother. "Mom?" I said. "Mom?"

My mother didn't answer.

I ate M&Ms and potato chips. I left the room and walked in a big circle. I saw a well-known actress leaning over the bed of her father.

I came back to where I started from. "Mom?" I said. "Mom?"

"Mom!" my mother said. "Mom!" She was mimicking me!

I laughed a laugh that had nothing to do with laughing. I asked my mother, "Are you mad at me?"

My mother said, "Why would I be mad?"

Gladiators

I'm dating my brother. At least it feels that way as I dress for lunch. Now that Mother is dead, my brother is the only one left with the power to give me that final thumbs-up, thumbs-down.

We've been estranged for a year. Everyone's been mad at everyone else—his wife, my husband, friends on the sidelines. He calls during that week between Christmas and New Year's, that out-of-time week, to suggest lunch. I check my jewelry to make sure I'm not wearing anything inflammatory.

Paulina is in the kitchen preparing her complicated Polish lunch. Paulina cleans my apartment on Thursdays. She looks me over. I'm wearing a certain pair of black pants and a certain black turtleneck sweater. I can tell

Paulina doesn't approve by the way the corners of her mouth tighten and her lips purse.

"No?" I say. I can't help myself.

"Mmm," she says. She gets very involved with a smudge on the side of the toaster.

Paulina leaves my underpants in the dictionary and floor lamps on top of tables. My brother's wife fired her after one day. If I were still seeing Dr. Gold, maybe I'd have a normal cleaning lady.

"Is it cold out?" I'm rummaging through the coat closet. Let her be that way.

"*Hawney,*" she pleads. She's followed me into the hall. "Why you don't wear beautiful shoes?" I'm wearing expensive rubber-soled shoes as plain as tires. Paulina's feminine ideal was shaped in response to the America of 1964 as seen from the point of view of a former Soviet bloc country. Mine was shaped in response to my mother as seen from the point of view of twenty years of psychotherapy.

The thing about me is I can't resist a thumbs-down no matter where it comes from. I change into stiletto-heeled boots, a skinny skirt, and clingy top.

Paulina beams when I come out of the bedroom. She claps her hands and shakes her head. Words fail her.

"It's just lunch," I say.

I pick up my purse and walk through the living room. The porcelain Foo Dogs that used to sit on my mother's hall table and now sit on mine are tucked into a corner of the sofa where Paulina ostentatiously moves them out of harm's way while she cleans. I notice that the snarling dog is missing a piece of its tail. I drop my purse and pick up the broken dog. Then I dig behind the seat cushion and extract the broken-off tip.

"Paulina?" I call out. When it came down to the dogs or a lithograph, I kept quiet and waited for my brother to choose. I've always loved these dogs. Paulina hurries over wearing the concerned look of the innocent bystander. I show her the dog.

"Who break!" she exclaims.

"*You* break," I tell her. I'm furious.

I see her trying to choose a strategy. "No! *How* I break?"

"How? You move too fast. You don't take care." This is well known and has been exhaustively documented over our six years together.

Paulina looks at the evidence in my hands, then at me. "Hawney. If I break, I hide."

When I walk out the door she's sitting on a chair against the wall, eating her lunch off an odd dish I haven't seen in years.

My brother stands in front of the restaurant smoking a cigarette. He's wearing an elegant overcoat but it looks slouchy. He's skinnier than ever. When we were kids in Ohio, he was clearly my younger brother, if only by three years. Then we grew up and he seemed like my older brother. Now that we are whatever we are it's hard to say. He's definitely my only brother. I get shy the second I spot him from way down the block. I cross the street toward him. I see him seeing me from behind his sunglasses. He doesn't smile.

We kiss cheeks.

"Did you see me?" I say. I'm in some kind of date flutter.

"I see you now," he says. He's not fluttering.

He holds out a small gift-wrapped package. "Merry Christmas." He says it sweetly.

"Oooh," I say. It has a promising heft.

"Don't get excited," he says.

It's a Japanese restaurant, the kind for Midtown businessmen. My brother didn't use to like Japanese food. When we're seated he tells me that the steak with three special dipping sauces is good.

I start unwrapping the package. He considers me.

"Long hair," he says.

"Well, longer." My brother never really compliments me. Once he said, "What happened to your acne?"

The waiter gives us menus, and we each order a different brand of beer.

I tear off the rest of the gift wrap. There are three CDs: Eric Clapton, Macy Gray, the soundtrack from *Magnolia*. I feel guilty. I sent him twelve months of pears from Harry and David. When was the last time my brother took the trouble to pick out a present for me? His wife always did the gift-shopping.

"Work?" I say.

"Bad."

Shorthand. Good sign. "Bad how?"

"We're moving our offices to New Jersey."

My brother is a political consultant. He was the first operative in Romania after Communism. Now he's doing something in Bolivia. Who knows where he learned that stuff.

"Well, you look good," I say. "Tan."

"Really? Anguilla, but months ago."

The upside of not speaking to my brother was not knowing how many times he and his wife have vacationed in the Caribbean. I don't know why I care.

He tells me that he gets altitude sickness in La Paz and has to sleep with an oxygen tank, that he and his wife are suing their decorator over a twenty-three-thousand-dollar rug, that the skylight in their loft still leaks every time it rains. Now that I see that the theme of the lunch is going to be how things fall apart, not four-star resort hotels, I relax.

"I'm still waiting to hear from the IRS on that Mother thing, although the attorney thinks we have a good spousal immunity case if they do flag it." This in reference to the business shenanigans of Percy Perry, the one who sprang us from the suburbs of the Midwest, the one Mother sold her soul to for college tuition and California and Manhattan. My brother's longtime contempt for Mother's last ex-husband now finds expression in the mastery of tax codes, the drafting of expensive legal correspondence, but the bitter taste in my mouth has its source, as always, in that deep spring of complicated love for Mother.

"It never ends," he says. He sighs. It's the same

kind of sigh Paulina sighs. It's an Eastern European sigh. I feel right at home in it.

"So do you think we should worry?" I'm just saying the words. While he analyzes our risk of inheriting a financial nightmare, I picture a bleak autumn Saturday when no one came to get us at the movies. We liked spectacles and disasters—lions and Christians, earthquakes and Martians, self-important biblical epics where the velvet curtains closed for Intermission. That darkening afternoon we were the last children left under the marquee when the wind lifted my brother's cap and sent it skittering across a busy highway. I chased the cap while some teenagers on the corner laughed. I still remember how frightened I felt when I turned and saw my little brother standing all alone in his bulky coat. One time he came down to the rec room where I was watching Daddy nap, childish arousal all over my face. *I know what you're doing*, my brother said. The thing about a brother? You live your whole life knowing there's a surprise witness waiting right outside the courtroom ready to testify. You just don't know which way.

We order lunch.

"Let me ask you something," I say. "Remember when we used to skate on the pond? Did I know how to skate backward?"

"You could do it, but not with any speed." God, I've missed him! He's my own personal Doris Kearns Goodwin.

"Was the pond as big as it seemed to us then,

do you think? Or was it a speck the whole time?" We haven't lived in Ohio for thirty years.

"I think it was a decent size. Big enough for hockey."

My brother was the better offensive player—bold on the attack, willing to take every reckless chance. He'd try to distract me with his wildman feints, jokes, and stunts, but I was a stoical goalie. I just planted myself and refused to let anything by.

"I saw a picture of a beautiful cemetery in East Hampton," I tell him. (You can skip transitions with my brother. No need to explain that my mind jumped to Mother's ashes. We'd thought of scattering them over the pond until I pointed out that she was afraid of water. We haven't come up with Plan B. As far as I know, the ashes are still on a shelf in my brother's closet.) "What I'm saying is—this cemetery, it was so *pretty*." What *am* I saying? Next thing you know I'll be flipping my hair around. "It made me think, well, maybe cremation isn't the way to go. If we were buried, we could all be together." I realize my mistake right away from the look on his face.

"But you and I wouldn't be together," he says. What kills me is he says it kindly. "Husbands and wives are together, not brothers and sisters."

The waiter sets down a box filled with sushi for me, some kind of mini-grill holding perfect slices of charred red beef for my brother.

"Yum," I say.

We order two more beers.

"So why did you invite me to lunch?" I feel the need to regain some older sister ground.

"I missed you." He sounds sincere.

"I missed you, too."

"You know, for a while I was shocked."

"Because . . . ?" I'm good at playing dumb. It's part of my interviewing technique.

"Ever since Mother got sick, people have been telling me stories. About what happens in families. Apparently, this thing between us is pretty common."

I make a noise indicating yes, people tell me stories, too.

"I just never imagined it could happen to *us*. I mean, I always thought of us as so close." He sounds genuine, the way he says it, like he never did imagine it. Like it was one way and now it's another way, like he was standing around and an asteroid fell out of the sky.

We're tragedy hounds, my brother and I. When the news is bad, we find each other first. Bobby Kennedy, Martin Luther King Jr., John Lennon, the Challenger. The weekend Princess Diana was killed? My brother and his wife were vacationing in Napa Valley, but every night he called me from the grounds of a different four-star inn. He'd smoke a cigarette and we'd discuss the day's emotional highs and lows. "I just can't believe it," one of us would say. "I know, it's unbelievable," the other would say. John Kennedy Jr.'s plane disappeared during the not-speaking time, but I knew my brother was plastered to cable like I was, thinking how it had always been the three of them, Jackie and those two kids.

My brother says, "Also, there's a business matter I need to discuss with you."

"You have an agenda?" I say.

He clears his throat. "Is there something wrong with that?"

I can't think of how to say everything that's wrong with it.

"I want to know if you have any problem with me taking an executor's fee. I ran it past the attorneys—they say that even when a family member is named executor, state law entitles them to a standard two percent."

He's looking directly at me, this neutral expression on his face, like he's actually hoping I'll feel invited to share my thoughts on the subject. He only breaks eye contact to transfer another piece of steak from the still sizzling grill to his plate. Brilliant. He's very good, my brother. I knew this man once who told me that for the New Year I should resolve to not let all my feelings show on my face.

"As you know, I've devoted a lot of hours to straightening out Mother's affairs over the past year, and there's all this tax business still ahead of us. So I think it's fair." He cuts a piece of steak. Dips it.

A scene from that movie *Julia* jumps into my head. Lillian Hellman is having drinks with friends, and someone says something stupid, about politics probably, and Jane Fonda overturns the table like a gunslinger in a saloon. That's what comes to mind. Something

117

muscular and clean, with broken glass. I feel like a ten-year-old in a spoiled party dress. I feel like everything is lost.

"What's the percentage for the person who spent the last three years with her in doctors' offices?" I ask my brother. "What's that worth?"

A week after Mother died, my brother and I arranged to spend an hour by ourselves in her apartment. That sunny afternoon was our first time together in those now stale rooms since some family dinner that already belonged, unfathomably, to the past. It pained me to see that the windows needed washing. We were very careful with each other. We made the big decisions without rancor or raised voices, indicating through murmur, shrug, and sidelong glance what we might want to keep, what we thought we'd sell or donate or give to friends. Then we began to focus, more gingerly, on objects. I quickly understood my brother's intention was to reclaim every gift he and his wife had ever given Mother. Silver candlesticks and Steuben glass snails, Tiffany picture frames, tiny Limoges boxes. Daughter-in-law gifts. When he presented me with a list of gift jewelry they expected me to return—I'd taken Mother's jewelry and furs to my apartment the day she was hospitalized—I said, "You're kidding, right?" I swear, he took a step toward me like he was going for my throat. I slammed the door behind me. (On the subway going home, I chortled like a demented person to see that their list included jewelry Mother had given to me years ago.) Why was my brother so mad at me? Did he think he could come between me and Mother's jewelry? What world did he live in? I asked myself if I had killed our mother. Was it possible I had done it but didn't remember doing it, like a character in one of her soaps? Was that it? Because no lesser explanation could account for the murder in his eyes. After that we took turns going there. On my days, I packed up closets and cupboards and carted home my own offerings—jaunty hand-painted French dessert plates, beaded African dolls, coffee-table books on women and art and the Holocaust. Daughter gifts. One afternoon I let myself into the apartment to discover our baby portraits removed from the wall, those sweet black and white photographs in oval frames that had hung next to each other on all the walls of all the houses, mine a little higher, his a little lower. I found my picture all by itself, stacked in a carton on top of some high school Latin notebooks I didn't know were still around. (*Mirabile dictu!* I'd written in balloon letters all over my Virgil. *Ave atque Vale!*) What kind of person does something like that?

"So you do have a problem with it?" my brother is saying. "Because I doubt you really know what's involved."

"What I know is that family members don't take executor's fees," I say. I marble each word with condescension. "Ever. That's something I know." My voice is black ice, even though I can feel my upper lip twitch with fury and my heart bang away beneath my curvy top. My hands get busy inside my purse,

119

efficiently marshaling lipstick and wallet and keys like they're already late for their next meeting. That's when I see uncertainty flicker in my brother's eyes. All at once I'm exultant, practically dizzy. I still have it, my ancient power to demolish my little brother with scorn—for his bad handwriting and violation of library quiet rules, for not understanding the difference between adjectives and adverbs, for tormenting the dog and wetting the bed, for jumping off the garage and using bad language, for making us rescue him from sleepaway camp and the emergency room and the police station, for finding the dirty pictures in their nightstand drawer, for scaring me in the shower and pinning me to the floor, for stonewalling and sleeping all day and reentering through Mexico, for getting away with it, for losing his stupid cap in the wind.

When the check comes, we each put down cash.

We part on the corner of Fifty-third Street, at the entrance to the subway. I don't go down the stairs right away. I watch the back of my brother's long coat make its way toward Madison, uptown in the direction of his office and the building where Mother used to live. I think, we're not even from here.

Paulina is ironing when I come in. "Nobody loves you!" she singsongs as I walk to my desk to check the answering machine.

I've limped all the way from the subway. When I pull off my boots, one of my heels is rubbed raw and bleeding.

I pad into the living room with my boots in one hand. I see that Paulina has tried to fix the broken Foo Dog. Now it lies precariously on its side on the dining room table. The open growly mouth looks silly. A book and a plant are propped against the dog to hold the pieces of the tail in place while the glue dries. You can see clearly where the break is. I glare at Paulina, go into my bedroom, close the door behind me. I take off my clothes, pull on sweat pants and a T-shirt, then get into bed and turn on *Oprah*. A sad-eyed man is explaining that life is a university and that romantic love is only one course at the university. He looks like a ventriloquist's dummy. "Oh, that's good," Oprah is saying. "That is really good." I can see out the window to the park, where the wind has trapped a shredded piece of red plastic bag high in the bare branches of the tallest tree. That bag has been stuck in that tree since last winter. I can't believe that bag is still there. That bag is a blight. How long is that bag going to hang on? I'm almost beginning to have respect for that bag. Maybe it's not a bag. Maybe it's a balloon that crash-landed in the tree. I think of the lipstick faces I used to draw on balloons when my brother and I played nightclub. We attached the balloon heads to Mother's long, silky nightgowns and took the balloon dates dancing. I hear the door close as Paulina leaves.

That evening my husband says, "So how was your day? Any good stories? Any interesting phone calls?" I don't tell him I had lunch with my brother. I just don't. My husband has a sister. She lives in London, so they don't see each other much, but they speak on the phone now and then. They have discussions. They exchange news about their aging parents, whom they refer to as "the folks." It's like another civilization, my husband's family, like a civilization you might read about in *National Geographic*. "Well, thanks a lot for calling!" he says to his sister. "It's really nice to talk to you."

On our way to bed, my husband spots the broken dog. "Hey. What happened to your mother's dog?" he says.

What's there to say? I could say, This is not right. I could say, My heart is broken. "Don't even get me started on that dog," I say. I march off to the bedroom as if he did get me started. I turn down the bed. When I start to draw the curtains closed, I hear the wind howling and glance up one more time at the Christmas sky. It's too dark to see the scrap of red, but I know it's there.

General Strike

It was almost Thanksgiving when I realized I'd made a terrible mistake. No one had invited us and we had invited no one.

"We could go to Europe," I told Richard. "We liked it there. Remember?"

We'd finished dinner—it was my week to cook and I'd made penne putanesca, Richard's favorite—and now he was rinsing the dishes, stacking them in the dishwasher in his careful, considered way. "You have to think like a dishwasher," he liked to remind me whenever the plates and glasses on my watch came out crusty or filled with water.

I was standing on the threshold of our tiny kitchen, with the television guide in my hand. The anniversary of the Kennedy assassination was coming up, and there was a full roster of specials on every single night this week. Last night I'd watched one about the President's various medical conditions. All the familiar, comforting names had been in it. Tuinal. Dexedrine. Ted Sorensen. It was about to be the fortieth anniversary of that day and I was getting ready to be sad in a slightly more inflated way than usual.

I hadn't been able to figure out where I was supposed to be on Thanksgiving ever since Mother died four years ago. There was the first Thanksgiving, or non-Thanksgiving, the one that my brother, Alex, and I had passed in the stunned hallways and hospital rooms of Mount Sinai Hospital. But the ones after that were a blur. Richard and I went to Brooklyn once, I was pretty sure I remembered that. And there was the Thanksgiving night when our new and intimidatingly sophisticated refrigerator loaded with leftovers came down with a mysterious ailment, when Richard and I stood before it, cocking our heads and listening for reassuring sounds, only to watch in helpless disbelief as the cabinet temperature continued to rise. Last year, I panicked and wound up with twenty people around my table. Phoebe and her extended family. Abby and her newly remarried mother. Gabe, Richard's middle son, came at the last minute with his girlfriend.

Not my brother. Alex and his wife, Suzanne, went to Rome that year, just as they had done every Thanksgiving since Mother died, as if all the years of all the Thanksgivings Alex and I had spent together, from childhood on into adulthood and middle age, had never happened. I'd rented tables and linens and stemware and bought garlanded napkin rings that looked pretty on Mother's turkey plates—there were exactly twenty of them. I'd cooked and baked, and Richard had done the cleanup, and everyone contributed and everything was delicious, especially the gravy, and for weeks Richard and I had made a special effort to use the words "pan juices" as often as possible. Rome!

I hadn't been to Rome since right after college, with Phoebe. Richard hadn't been there since childhood. He and I didn't travel often. Is that what happened when you grew up in a Navy family? He'd lived all over the world by the time he was fifteen. Now he preferred to stay put. But when we did go away, Richard was the best kind of traveler—curious and self-sufficient, eager to learn the transportation system, willing to rise early to buy bread and cheese at the market, patiently reading every word on every little museum card, every date on every village monument.

I was the one who grumbled about how we never seemed to go anywhere. All I really wanted out of being somewhere else was a glimpse of the past—anyone's past, any monument to anyone's past. Inevitably, the past eluded me. Then the only thing that could soothe me was a luxurious hotel, one with a wonderful bathroom.

"Remember Paris?" I told Richard. "We loved Paris." We'd spent a week there on the solemn occasion of my fiftieth birthday, staying at a hotel that had once been Gestapo headquarters—an excellent hotel. Then we took an overnight train to Prague, one that left from the Gare de l'Est, the most atmospherically sinister train station in Paris.

Oh, the past was tantalizingly close during that trip. I spent most of it trying to imagine being alive in the world of 1941, or at least in a Hitchcock movie from the period or, failing that, in a John le Carré novel about a slightly less dangerous but still menacing time. Now even I had to admit, there was excellent food and an ominous atmosphere right here in New York. Why travel?

"What about the boys?" Richard said. "We still don't know what they're doing for Thanksgiving."

Richard's ex-wife in St. Louis would get one, possibly two of their grown boys. But maybe it wasn't too late to snag one for ourselves. Wasn't Thanksgiving supposed to be the holiday when the music stopped, when whatever family you had was the family around your table? "Call them," I said. "Call them right now."

Neither my brother nor I had children of our own. Was that why Thanksgiving hadn't outlasted Mother? Our only surviving ritual at this time of year was remembering the Kennedy assassination. It went unmentioned the first year after Mother's death, of course. All exchanges between Alex and me during that terrible time were rageful and accusatory, followed by rude hang-ups and hostile e-mail. I'd had to make a special appointment to see Dr. Gold to discuss it. I hadn't seen her since Richard and I married. Her office was still on that beautiful block, by the museum. She looked the same. That is, she looked the same ten years older than I was that she had always looked. We hugged, self-consciously, and I felt disoriented by the extreme close-up view of her nose and pores. I'd brought an angry e-mail Alex had sent me and waited for Dr. Gold to read it. Her face registered the right amount of shock and concern. I looked around the office. The same good African art, the same tasteful tapestries. I watched her face grow more serious. That was good. Once she had finished reading, though, I had the old familiar feeling: What more was there to say?

"Well, he certainly is angry," she said.

After two years of bitterness, Alex and I entered into a cautious telephone détente, triggered in part by a tearful telephone reliving one morning of Jimmy Smits's tragic death on *NYPD Blue* the night before.

Now when we spoke, it was about his dismal work situation. The small PR company he'd been with for years had recently been acquired by a large European group. The two hundred e-mails before lunch, the more senior partners handsomely bought out; the new partners, younger by twenty years; worst of all, the revised job title with its ageist whiff of demotion. Alex was obsessed with someone from the new group named Hart. "He works hard, he's prolific, but he's a dunderhead, a bean counter." Was Hart a first name or a last? I murmured sounds of comfort. "I see very clearly that Hart will always see me the way he sees me, Grace, that he will never see me any other way." Really, it was getting to be a sickness, this Hart fixation.

"He will always want to keep me in my place. The fact is, people there like me and they don't like Hart."

"Don't worry so much. I'm sure it'll get better. Let go of work a little bit." It hurt my heart to hear Alex so demoralized. I was the older sister. I felt responsible. It was up to me. I remembered the time Alex jumped into a snowdrift on our walk to school one morning. We were little kids. He got stuck in the drift, and I couldn't pull him out. The rest of the kids disappeared into school, then the bell rang, and I still couldn't get him out. For a minute there I was pretty certain we were the last children on earth. Finally, I got up the nerve to walk back to a gas station and get a man with a shovel to come and dig him out. For an older sister I was boss, but I didn't even have the basic common sense.

"What's the worst thing that can happen?" Alex had said in a recent call, temporarily philosophical. A Hart rant had freed him briefly of the man's awful hold on him. "Suzanne and I will sell the apartment."

While Richard retreated to the bedroom to call his boys, I trotted down the hall to retrieve the Williams-Sonoma holiday catalogue from the recycling box.

On my way out I had to admire, as always, the beautiful paint job in the foyer. On this night, my admiration was undercut by worry. All the wiring, so neatly and painstakingly concealed by that fine Bulgarian craftsman, was destined to be wrecked tomorrow morning by the cable guy. But what choice did I have? As soon as I saw the coming week's schedule of assassination programming, I had to order the device that allowed you to record many shows at once. "It's an emergency," I'd explained to the service representative after holding for twenty minutes.

Richard and I had used some of the Mother money to redo our kitchen, then last year put a chunk more into repainting the entire apartment, a project that had turned out to be almost as costly as the kitchen renovation. "It's our own fault," I told Richard whenever he remembered how much the painter was charging. "We didn't prepare the walls correctly when we moved in. We didn't skim coat." Luckily, at the sound of the words "skim coat" Richard's eyes went into a coma expression, and he quickly changed the subject.

Only Court TV had that same tranquilizing effect on me. Every other television show hurled me back into the trivial, traumatic maintenance issues that had taken over my life in this, the frightening late middle of it, ruining the whole point of television. Wooden blinds, for example. The same ones that covered the windows in the television West Wing of the White House and in the television offices of various district attorney offices covered the window in my study. No plot could compete with my interest in those television blinds. Suddenly I'd be violently thrown out of the story. Were the television blinds painted? Were they natural wood? Distressed? How wide were they? What color was the fabric tape? Plain or patterned? In other words, had I made an irreversible mistake? Wasn't the whole point of television to provide a respite from this kind of self-recrimination? No matter how marginally interesting the crime, how dismal the courtroom, how badly dressed the witnesses and attorneys, so far everyone I'd seen on Court TV had made mistakes that were bigger than mine. I had yet to see a courtroom with blinds.

When I returned from the recycling room, I went online and ordered a free-range turkey from the catalogue. Then I poked my head into the bedroom. The television was on mute, and Richard was just hanging up the phone. "The boys are all spoken for. Looks like we're on our own, babes." But he didn't seem sad. Not in an inflated or in uninflated way.

A few nights later, I called Alex to review the recent assassination programming. On the conspiracy channel, a fat articulate woman had claimed to have been Lee Harvey Oswald's lover in New Orleans. She said she was recruited by Oswald to help concoct a cancer drug to kill Fidel Castro. The woman spoke, we agreed, with heartfelt emotion about Oswald. In her account, he was innocent. Several times she had to ask the interviewer to stop so that she could collect herself. On a network channel a familiar anchorman told the life story of Oswald, a story in which there was no lover and no heartfelt emotion and no plot to kill Castro and, most of all, no question of innocence. Another night, Larry King had hosted the last living eyewitness from the death car itself, reading for the first time ever from the diary she'd kept of that day. So do you still think about it? Larry had asked her.

"Maybe that's the thing about the fortieth anniversary," Alex said. "People start to say things. They realize that pretty soon they'll all be dead."

I was feeling so relieved that we were getting through an entire conversation without a mention of the Hart situation, I almost missed what Alex said next. "You and Richard should come to Rome with us this year. You should. Really. We'll have fun."

"We could go to Italy," I told Richard that same evening. "You love Italy." It was his week to cook, and he'd started off with fish tacos, which we were eating in front of a History Channel documentary that maintained Lyndon Johnson's shady business associates had masterminded the Kennedy assassination. Richard barely tolerated such shows; I wasn't so crazy about fish tacos. We were in the middle of our marriage. "I mean, we could go to Rome with Alex and Suzanne."

"If we went to Italy, would you make us stay with Alex and Suzanne in an expensive hotel?" Richard said.

I thought about my husband flying thousands of miles to stare at the ruined past through the windows of the same designer boutiques and expensive restaurants that he preferred to avoid in the crumbling unaffordable present. I'd read somewhere that the key to a happy marriage was secretly suspecting your mate of being a finer person than you were. Or maybe I had interviewed someone who had said those words. I thought about Alex and Suzanne, about the four of us growing old together, about being a family that celebrated Thanksgiving together, in Rome.

"Yes," I said. And I canceled the turkey.

It was raining in Rome, and the taxi driver informed us that the weather would remain the same through the weekend, adding that rain made the Romans very sad. But once we'd checked into our adjoining rooms—Suzanne had booked us into their usual hotel at the top of the Spanish Steps—and more or less unpacked, the four of us reset our watches like seasoned travelers and took our jet lag right back out into the wet Italian morning.

Two by two, we walked the narrow cobblestone streets, past the glossy boutiques, dodging cars and motorbikes and other people's umbrellas. Rome was pink and old and even on a gray rainy day a thousand times righter–looking, I thought, than any American city I could think of besides New York.

Richard wanted to see the Trevi Fountain, and since we had no particular agenda other than to walk off our jet lag, we headed there. The four of us stood in the rain and stared at the water gushing over marble. We threw as many coins as we could find over our shoulders, but the ritual insuring return was made cumbersome by umbrellas and cameras, and further complicated by the aggressive street vendors trying to thrust roses into our hands.

Mother was there. I could see her in black and white, sitting on the edge of this very fountain with Percy, just as she existed in my photo album. Mother on her final honeymoon, in a well-cut white suit, Jackie O sunglasses, and her new nose. That first time I'd traveled around Europe, I couldn't see anything. No matter what I looked at—Michelangelo, the Louvre, a canal in Venice, Mother was in the way. Now she was more like one of those dark unformed apparitions I'd begun spotting out of the corner of my eye. Floaters, the young ophthalmologist called them. "It's a natural part of aging," he'd said matter-of-factly. Alex and I exchanged a look. Good, he saw her, too.

"Is anyone interested in lunch?" Richard wanted to know.

"We could eat at Nino's," I said, instinctively looking toward Alex for approval. I remembered the restaurant from that long-ago trip with Phoebe. "Is it still there?"

"Still there," Alex said. "Still the same."

We wound our way through a different warren of streets and soon spotted the green sign, below it the restaurant I remembered from a long time ago.

I tugged at Richard's arm. "Sweetie, this is the place I told you about." I had eaten a transporting bowl of tortellini al brodo here.

The waiter led us to a table against one wall, and as we dutifully followed him through the buttery room, fragments of Italian melodically floated up from the tables. We hung our dripping jackets and umbrellas and sank into the tall menus the waiter offered, everyone pretending to ignore the English translations printed on one side.

It was good, if earthbound, and as we lingered over espressos, Alex took out his pack of cigarettes. You could still do that here. I remembered the time in my early thirties when Mother and I took Italian lessons.

"Mother took Italian lessons?" Alex said.

"*Portacenere* was the one vocabulary word she could remember. She loved saying it. It drove me crazy." The word for ashtray, but she delivered it as if pledging eternal love to Marcello Mastroianni. "She couldn't do the grammar. It was shocking. Painful. Pitiful. We dropped out after three lessons." Mother had been paying for the tutor. She'd wanted us to like each other. I was good at the grammar and the vocabulary. But the way Mother said that one word, *portacenere*! Well, I couldn't do that then and I still couldn't do it.

Now I was reminded of Mother's actual ashes— not in a *portacenere* but in a canister in a Bergdorf Goodman shopping bag on a top shelf of Alex's closet. They'd been there for four years. Mother loved Rome. We could have brought the ashes to Rome.

"And do what?" Alex said when I mentioned it. "Scatter them in Fendi?"

Suzanne, reapplying a perfectly neutral shade of lipstick in a ballet of intricately expert small-motor movements, stopped mid-lip to laugh. Alex still made her laugh.

Richard looked confused and a little bit Catholic.

But wasn't scattering ashes the kind of thing families did, even nonobservant Jewish families like ours? Scattering ashes would have given the trip a purpose beyond sightseeing and shopping and eating in restaurants. At least it wasn't touristy. Or was it? I'd heard of a parent scattered in Paris, another in the Grand Canal in Venice. I was thinking along the lines of the Protestant Cemetery, the pretty green place I remembered seeing with Phoebe, where Keats and Shelley were buried. But what did that have to do with Mother? The Jewish Ghetto? No.

Alex caught the waiter's eye to ask for the check. I felt spinny, or tipsy. I felt sad. I rested my head on Richard's shoulder. I tried to detach from the feeling, to remember that I always felt sad my first day away from home. But I could already make out the familiar outlines of disappointed-in-myself, plus the panicky feeling that I had packed all the wrong books. I straightened up.

"Do you think anyone our age has fun anymore?" I said. Maybe fun was only possible the first time you traveled. Everything was a miracle then, starting with the fact that you'd managed to leave home at all.

No one had an opinion.

The check arrived, and as credit cards were produced, Alex gave me an appraising look. "Try to get a grip," he said. "It's only our first day."

"*Grazie! Grazie!*" everyone murmured as we made our way out, and we were released to the wet streets again.

I realized that Thanksgiving had come and gone.

∧ ∧ ∧

Workmen on ladders were attaching miniature Santas to the facade of the hotel when we returned. We separated for naps, sleep disquieting and mystical.

I woke at four—was it afternoon or the middle of the night? I was shivering. They had pushed two twins together for us, but a gap of an inch or two remained, a sliver of space that appeared to me now as wide as the Continental Divide. Richard's bed was empty. I got up and closed the door against the rain drizzling on the small terrace. Then I found my way through the darkened room to the bathroom. Light blazed through the crack of the door. There was Richard, reading in the tub, its chilly porcelain cushioned by a pile of thick white towels. He was naked.

"Sweetie? Aren't you cold?" It was an alternate history of World War II. A literary page-turner.

"I'm fine." He sounded fine. "You know, I think you'd enjoy this book. It doesn't have time travel, but it does have Hitler."

"Come to bed," I whispered. Two fluffy white hotel bathrobes hung side by side on hooks near the tub, belts neatly tied.

By the next morning, our jet lag was gone, and the Roman sun seemed to be making an effort. Richard had gone out for a run. I was just calling room service when he came in.

"Should I order you a cappuccino?"

"No thanks. Look what I got." He dropped a wet plastic bag on the bed, then went to the bathroom to towel off. "I tried getting you a cappuccino to go but I guess they don't do that here," he called out.

Was the line ringing on the other end or was this the busy signal? I'd already heard room service come and go from Alex and Suzanne's room. I stared dubiously into the bag. A hunk of Parmigiano-Reggiano and half a pound of prosciutto stared back at me. I pictured Alex in the next room, guiltlessly drinking the last of his foamy coffee, reading the paper, lazily preparing himself for a shower. All I wanted was a cup of coffee, on a tray, with a little roll!

"*Buon giorno!* Room service!" said the operator at last.

"I'm sorry, never mind," I said and hung up the phone.

Our foursome decided to separate for the day. Alex and Suzanne were going to shop, leaving Richard and me to sightsee.

The concierge informed us solemnly that today there would be a General Strike, which seemed among other things to have something to do with the unavailability of taxis. He offered to call a car. But Richard had already scoped out the metro station on his run. We descended into the gloom of the underground passages, fed coins into a machine for tickets, then studied the turnstiles, trying to figure out what we were supposed to do with the tiny pieces of paper. Graffiti was everywhere. The train pulling in was covered with it.

"*This* is time travel," I said. "New York in the seventies."

But my spirits were rising. We had successfully navigated the subway, and though we had to stand helplessly in a long, inefficient line to buy our tickets at an understaffed entrance to the Colosseum, we happily walked most of its circumference, then climbed to the third tier. We were leaning on the blackened stone staring out at the arena, where the restoration of the floor appeared to be halfway finished. You could still see the corridors and tunnels carved into the ground below. How could anyone keep up with the present when the past was such a burden to maintain? Why not knock the whole thing down? Maybe the problem was too *much* respect for the past.

"Were the ancient Romans good or bad?" I asked Richard.

"Well . . ." he began. He knew, sort of, and he would explain, eventually, but our brains were on permanently different time zones and mine was already skipping ahead.

I remembered hearing our own president answer the question of how he imagined the people of the future would judge him. "We'll never know," he'd said. "We'll all be dead." I had been stunned to hear a president say exactly the kind of thing I said to myself when I was feeling my most futureless. But instead of thinking, Yes, exactly! I thought the opposite. People were always remembering to say how important it was to remember the past, then they went ahead and forgot it. Wasn't it just as important to remember the future?

138

The president was a father. Weren't children supposed to be the bridge to that place?

When I tried to translate the Latin engraved on the marble, all I could remember were the cases— nominative, genitive, dative, accusative, ablative. Richard teased me by orating the last line of the prize-winning poem I'd written in Latin class the year JFK was murdered. "Thank you, John John, for saluting," he said. I screwed up my face in embarrassment. "Hey, you made a silly face," he said appreciatively. "You don't usually do that. "

We drank espressos. Two old men at the next table shook their heads at a group of protesters on the other side of the plaza. One said to the other, *"Solo prolonga la miseria."*

I repeated it to Richard as we wandered back toward the hotel, stopping to buy pears and apples at a market stall. *"Solo prolonga la miseria,"* I said. I said it thoughtfully and then I said it with hand gestures and then with melancholy Italian existential angst. I wondered what exactly it was that only prolonged the misery. Was it the strike? More important, what was the misery? What I loved most was the *only*. Back in the hotel room, Richard and I sat on the bed and ate the fruit with the cheese and prosciutto. I couldn't imagine a more delicious lunch.

In the afternoon we walked to the Vatican, moving obediently with the flow of other visitors through long corridors filled with tapestries, frescoes, and sculptures. So many rosy infants being handed to, or was it wrested from, so many outstretched arms. So much violence and grief. I didn't get religion. I wasn't a parent. I had put my faith in the wrong things—psychology and novels.

Richard's guidebook expressed the hope that we had brought "a good pair of binoculars, or at least a decent-sized mirror" to view the famous chapel's ceiling. We hadn't. We just stood there, looking up. What I saw was beautiful, it was ravishing—it was certainly cleaner than the first time I saw it—and I could see that a person could be deeply moved by it, but not me. I was going with, *Solo prolonga la miseria.*

That night we had arranged to meet Alex and Suzanne at a restaurant in Trastevere for dinner. I'd planned the evening to be a surprise for Alex. I'd made copies of childhood photographs he loved. I'd put them into a small album, almost identical to the original album I had.

I planned to wear one of my fanciful new tops (chiffon, some spangly stuff, pleats and tucks as intricate as that on a Japanese kimono) over jeans. I'd bought the top online, the same day I'd canceled the turkey. What happened was, I'd stumbled across a story about the Kennedy women and, as I was reading it, a link cunningly positioned in the margins of the text caught my eye. The link was the name of a fashionable clothing designer whose dresses and party wear I had often coveted despite the fact that I didn't live a life in which those clothes applied. When I clicked on the name, I was redirected to a cyber-boutique featuring not only that particular designer whose beautiful clothes didn't apply to my life but other designers, some whose beautiful clothes applied even less. By the end of that week four large boxes had been air-expressed to my New York apartment from London, with duty forms in triplicate. As people who commit adultery often say, "I didn't plan it. It just happened."

Dressing for dinner, I thought about how glad I was that the bad times, the weeks and months after Mother's death, were in the past for Alex and me. Thinking about Mother, though, turned out to be a bad direction. What came to mind were the dozen or more pairs of off-white trousers—flannel, gabardine, wool—I'd found hanging in one of her closets when I cleaned out her apartment after her death. Mother was a believer. Her own parents had rowed themselves across the Black Sea so that she could be a Jewish girl in Cleveland, not Odessa. How could she *not* believe in the future? Those trousers were articles of faith—that her life could, at any moment, take a turn that would include lunch with the Kennedys on Cape Cod or tea with Claudette Colbert on Barbados or, at the very least, dinner with the Ralph Laurens, or even just a quick bite on the Upper East Side with some people wearing his clothes. My own closet probably held an equal number of black pants, but it had never contained that much belief.

"You look glamorous," Richard said when I had finished dressing. (With my teeth, I'd ripped off the large tag on the delicate piece of chiffon that stated thrillingly, NO RETURNS WILL BE ACCEPTED

WITHOUT THIS TAG ATTACHED.) I felt a little glamorous.

I tried not to think about the misery that would be prolonged when I attempted to pay for that feeling. A magazine editor had called me up and asked me to write a story about how married couples had to constantly renegotiate their relationship. Just hearing the words "renegotiate" and "relationship" travel over the telephone line had caused the futureless feeling to come over me. I'd had to lie down until *Oprah* came on. Well, I would call the editor back. I would renegotiate. I looked in the mirror one last time and saw that I looked exactly like myself. If only I could exercise more authority with my cleaning lady, stop longing for things, and love the family I had, maybe I could begin to feel guilty about the right things.

Richard and I arrived at the restaurant first. Suzanne had made the reservation. "We don't want to be put upstairs with the other tourists," she had instructed the concierge with brusque authority. Suzanne was an attorney and unafraid to order people around. *Si, signora,* the concierge had replied deferentially. Speaking authoritatively to service personnel was another trait I hadn't mastered. If only my cleaning lady spoke Italian. *Si, signora. Prego.*

The maître d' seated us with a chilly flourish, after which no one appeared to offer us a drink. Richard paged through his little language dictionary to look up martini. It wasn't like Alex or Suzanne to be late. They were organized and prompt. Ten minutes passed. So much for Roman hospitality.

"Should we worry?" I asked Richard.

He turned the pages of the dictionary. *"Non lo so—"* More turning. *". . . esattamente."*

We hadn't run into any particular traffic. What was a General Strike, anyway? I quickly reviewed my brother's most recent health crises: a high, undiagnosable fever the first summer of West Nile virus, the recurring pinched nerve between C1 and 3 that had caused them to cancel last year's trip to Barcelona, the mysterious fainting episode at Suzanne's client's Christmas party after a single sip of red wine. Alex had been a guest of the emergency room since childhood.

When they appeared, with an apologetic story about a reunion with their longtime salesman at Armani, a waiter hurried over with menus and a wine list, pencil poised over pad, his eyes continuing to weigh and measure each movement in the room beyond us.

"Is that Mother's?" Alex said when I shrugged off my coat.

I told him it was mine.

"It's beautiful," Suzanne said.

"What did you two buy?" I asked her. Suzanne had found a way to eat Rome's version of the Zone Diet at every meal.

"Nothing fits me," said Suzanne. "Anyway, your brother was the one who needed to update."

"Two suits, a cashmere jacket, three sweaters. Shirts," Alex said matter-of-factly.

"Richard and I stopped at that little glove store near the hotel," I said. I sensed Richard and Suzanne beginning to apply themselves to the laborious work of conversation.

"No shopping for Richard?" Alex asked me.

"You know Richard hates to shop." I heard the snap in my voice. Richard was as famous for not wanting to shop as Suzanne was for not tolerating bad cleaning personnel. What was his point? I tried not to get into a bad mood.

Richard and Suzanne had moved from an account of our respective days to the price of real estate in TriBeCa, where my brother and sister-in-law lived in neutral splendor.

"I was just telling Richard what the Kaymans' loft sold for," Suzanne said to Alex. She turned to me. "The couple who bought it are thirty years old."

"All cash," Alex said. "He's a lawyer and I can't remember what she does. I think she just had her bat mitzvah."

"Their daughter?" Richard said, a beat behind.

The waiter came to take our wine order and recite the specials.

Everyone in this restaurant seemed to know everyone else, and the cheek kissing and table-hopping were like a foreign film without the subtitles. A comedy? A tragedy? The men were all slightly ridiculous-looking, in closely tailored double-vented jackets, and the women seemed to be whispering together about whose mistress was or was not here. Who were these people? Didn't they have to get up for work in the morning?

"By the way, are you recording?" Alex asked me when the waiter brought the little artichokes we now required at every meal. He meant the assassination shows. We remembered the assassinated president better than we remembered our own real father.

"I hope so," I said.

"Hope? Why hope? Don't you have TiVo?"

"Sort of. Well, something like it. No. I mean, yes." It was the day Paulina came to clean our apartment. I calculated the time difference. Who knows what damage she could be doing to the new recording box the cable company had installed.

"Did you schedule the Sunday night show I told you to watch?" He meant the one about the sixties, the one where something iconic and boomery happened before every commercial break. Civil rights! Vietnam! *American Bandstand*!

"That show. It's just too—something." I wished I could like it more. I could use a Sunday night show.

"But her character is exactly my age," Alex said persuasively. "The older brother is exactly your age. Even the theme music makes me cry."

"Well, she *is* excellent, that actress," I conceded. I wished I had something to make me cry. Then I remembered my American Express bill.

"They're doing one about the assassination this week," Alex said. Richard and Suzanne were still valiantly trying. Oh, let them take care of themselves.

I told Alex, "That was the beginning of everything going wrong." I wanted to make up for the Richard remark. One wrong turn and I knew he would be ruminating about Hart again. "Not just the big things, either. Remember how before that time a family would think nothing of walking into a movie theater together after the picture had already started, then would stay for the next show, to see the part they'd missed?"

Alex laughed. It was a sound almost identical to pain. He wiped tears from his eyes. "Yes!" he said. "Exactly."

"'I think this is where we came in,' mothers and fathers and brothers and sisters whispered to each other," I continued. I could always tell Alex a good story.

"We did that, remember? At the Stillwell Theater." Was Alex remembering our real father or our second father? At least Hart was vanquished for now.

The waiter came back with three different pastas.

"Uncle Sol died one week before Kennedy was killed," Alex told Suzanne and Richard as if continuing a conversation already launched. No one has a family as convincing as your own.

"What did he die of again?" Richard said to be polite.

"Heart attack," Alex and I said in unison. Mother's brother was the same age Alex was now.

"Remember tops?" Alex asked me.

I turned to Richard. "Sweetie, I told you about tops, didn't I?"

Uncle Sol owned a machine tool factory, a place somewhere on the mysterious outskirts of Cleveland.

The kids served as the off-site, pint-sized assembly line. Our five cousins griped about having to spend Saturdays bundling newspapers and folding stiff blue and white cardboard slabs with Blue Banner's zippy blue logo into boxes. Alex and I liked to work. We worked on the breezy side porch of their house or, on rainy days, the damp basement. We worked for the pleasure of it, for the novelty, for the lovely monotony.

"Tops were one part Tweety Bird–yellow plastic stem," I said. "One part strawberry-Twizzler-colored plastic disc." My cousin Rachel and I stacked 45s on the turntable—"Earth Angel," "Rockin' Robin," "Chantilly Lace"—before settling in for an hour or so of scooping, snapping together (sometimes chewing) the parts, then tossing each finished top into a carton. Scoop, snap, toss, plunk.

"What *were* tops, anyway?" I asked Alex now. I'd never thought to wonder before now. Tops were tops.

"They were the plastic things that closed the oil cans."

"You're kidding!"

"Uncle Sol loved me," Alex said.

We finished our pastas, and as soon as the waiter removed our plates I reached into my bag and removed the gift. I placed it on the table in front of Alex.

"What's this?" he said. He looked delighted. He unwrapped the small photo album. I could tell by his face that he completely got it. "It's the brown book!"

Suzanne and Richard looked happy and expectant, too.

"It's an exact copy of every picture," I said. Everyone at the table had seen the original brown book many times.

Alex had taken off his glasses and was turning the album's pages. Like me, he knew each photograph by heart. A professional photographer had come to the house one day when we were six and three. He photographed just Alex and me: getting dressed, coloring at the kitchen table, sitting on the sofa with toys, standing on a stool in order to brush our teeth at the bathroom sink, in bed together in flannel pajamas with feet, the pretend end of a long childhood day. We'd always loved the brown book.

"God. Thank you," Alex said. Suzanne beamed. "Baby, it's the brown book," he told her. I felt happy and relieved.

"I added some extra pictures at the end," I said then.

I waited for Alex to get to them. They were the biggest part of the surprise. Four black and white photographs taken on a small square of a front lawn. Our real father's sister had sent them to me, out of the blue. Alex and I and are in bathing suits. Mine has stars and moons on it. We're smiling little-kid smiles. Our real father, the man we call Irv, kneels between us, in a white T-shirt and khakis. He looks like Alex looked when he was in his twenties. Alex's lean little body leans against Irv's. My suntanned arm curls around Irv's neck. We'd never seen photographs of us with Irv.

"I have no memory of this," Alex said. "Where were these taken?"

"I think it was probably a Fourth of July weekend." I'd worked this out carefully in my mind when the pictures came. I'd explained it to Richard. "We must be at Irv's house," I told Alex. "Wherever he was living right after he and Mother separated."

"Really?"

"I'm pretty sure it was the weekend of the Sam Sheppard murder," I continued. I was guessing, really. But it could be true, couldn't it? I remembered the headlines from that weekend. I had just learned to read the newspaper.

"Wow," Suzanne said. "That gives me chills."

Alex and I had been obsessed with that hometown murder. Did the doctor kill his wife or did someone else do it? We'd read all the books. We'd watched every episode of *The Fugitive*. It was only recently that I'd begun to think about the little boy asleep in his bedroom while his mother was being murdered. That little boy had grown up. He was our age now. He had lost his mother and his father back there in the black and white fifties.

Alex was shaking his head. He looked dumbfounded. "I think I spent every Fourth of July holiday in my room, being punished," he said. "I can see myself, staring out the window at the empty street."

We finished two bottles of wine and drank liberally from the bottle of limoncello the waiter left on the table, and even though it was drizzly and the owner had offered to call a car, the four of us chose to walk back to the hotel, two by two.

When Richard and I got back to the room, I filled out the room service card for tomorrow's breakfast—one cappuccino, biscotti—while Richard flipped through the TV channels. I held up the long card. "You have to think like a tourist," I told him.

I opened the door to hang the card on the doorknob and glimpsed the tail end of a clothing rack being whisked by an invisible underling into Alex's room. Suzanne had made Armani promise to have the alterations by the end of the day.

I woke before light, crossed the divide, and crawled into Richard's arms.

"Sweetie, I think I might be sick," I said. My throat was a little raw, my limbs aching. Maybe I just needed a massage.

"Oh, no," Richard said. He rearranged himself around me. "You do feel hot."

When I woke again, Richard was pulling on his clothes. A sweater he'd owned since college, a pair of jeans. He would walk down the four flights of stairs rather than take the elevator. He would politely decline help with his bags. He would refuse to claim any special privilege. Who was he? I had married a stranger. I had married someone who wasn't anyone in my family.

Richard was putting his wallet into his pocket. "I'll

go to Nino's and make them wrap up some soup for you," he said.

"No, don't," I said. "*Please* don't. Have a day. Walk through the Borghese Gardens. Go back to the Vatican. You never got to see the Pietà."

I wanted to read my book. I wanted a massage. I wanted a long hot bath and room service. As soon as I heard voices next door, I picked up the phone. Suzanne answered. I said I wasn't feeling so hot.

"Wait. I'll put your brother on." Suzanne didn't do small talk. "You two really are a pair."

"What's wrong?" I said when Alex came on.

"Neck. It must have happened when I was trying on one of the new jackets. I moved an inch in the wrong direction. I'm bad. I can't turn my head without excruciating pain. My left arm is useless, and four fingers are numb, with some tingling in my thumb." He sighed. Even as a child he had found pleasure in the lengthy recitation of his symptoms. It wasn't enough for you to know his throat was sore—he wasn't satisfied until you had examined the redness for yourself, in the proper light, counted the stitches, placed your palm against his forehead.

He said that Suzanne was going to the Borghese Gallery, and maybe Richard wanted to go with her, but Richard had already picked up the gist from my end and was indicating no, no, absolutely not, and I made his apologies.

I woke next to the sound of a vacuum in the corridor outside. Richard was gone. There was my breakfast tray on the table across the darkened room. Richard must have let room service in. I remembered the housekeeper unlocking the door, her mumbled apology, then quiet again as she retreated. Was it afternoon or evening? I could make out the comforting murmur of television from next door.

My throat felt better. I got out of bed and, wrapping myself in the terrycloth robe, dropped the room card into a deep pocket. When I cracked open the door and peered into the corridor, it was quiet and empty. I slipped out, shutting the door behind me, and tapped on my brother's door. "It's me," I said.

Alex opened the door. He was wearing the same terrycloth robe. The hotel doctor had given him a neck brace, giving his head the appearance of a buoy bobbing on a white wave. He looked like a boy and a man. He looked like the father we could barely remember from childhood. At the same time, he looked like that same father when we next knew him, in his own late middle age. My brother looked like himself, like the person I loved most in the world.

"Are you watching TV?" he said. "You have to see this."

I followed him into the darkened room. The bed was convalescent neat, with a heating pad on it, and the pillows were plumped and smoothed. On the table next to the bed was an icepack, Advil, a cappuccino, a bag of pretzels, some chocolate from the minibar. Except for the pack of cigarettes and the *portacenere*, Alex ran a good sick room.

We arranged ourselves comfortably on the bed—

we happened to be wearing four-star terrycloth but we might as well have been in the matching pajamas with feet from the brown book—and turned our attention to the TV. We watched. This was our Rome, our Vatican, our Communion, our Sistine Chapel, our Chanukah, our Sabbath, our sacred ritual, our mourning, our ruins, our relic, our forgotten sadness, our ancient history, our rite. We would have crawled inside the television if we could. We would have eaten it whole.

"Pretzels?" Alex said. He passed them over.

The commentary— hushed, melodic, respectful— was in Italian, but the muffled drums that followed the caisson didn't need a translation and we knew the bagpipers and the wildly jerking horse as well as we knew the veiled widow and the fatherless children, one a little older, one a little younger. We knew it in any language, by heart.

We fluffed up pillows behind us, and settled back, letting the past cover us like a blanket. Now and then, one of us sighed loudly or said, Do you believe it? or offered the other a palmful of M&Ms. Then we returned to our joint task, nodding our heads to the sound of long familiar music, and watching, and though I thought about what Richard might be doing and what else was in the minibar and ordering lunch and whether there might be a good movie on next, I was happy to feel sad with my brother alongside me. I didn't feel bored or empty or afraid. I wanted to stay right there, watching the black and white pageant repeat itself and move on, repeat itself and move on, forever.

The Best Place to Be

We were walking home from a play, a comedy-drama about the tangled marital lives of people with kitchen equipment and summer arrangements similar to our own. "It's magic time," my husband had whispered into my ear as the curtain went up. My husband always did this. He claimed it was something Jack Lemmon used to say. Then he fell into a deep sleep, another theater tradition, for the entire first act. My rage had finally cooled.

I asked my husband if he wanted to participate in a research study about marriage. A magazine editor had called me up that day and asked me to write about it.

"Would I have to talk about myself?" my husband said. He had a look of misery on his face.

"I think we'd have to talk about a specific marriage issue," I told him.

What were our issues? Sex? We either had enough or too little. Way too little or just too little enough? Children? We had no children. Money? Suddenly our marriage seemed filled with issues.

I told him the name of the study. "How Couples Can Form Non-Patriarchal Bonds of Intimacy." My husband was silent. That had been my reaction exactly. I was stunned to hear the word *patriarchy* spoken unironically.

"Look at that building," my husband said. "Did you ever notice the top of that building?"

Apparently he wasn't stunned. He wasn't even listening. He was pointing at a building near Kiehl's Pharmacy, where I buy hair conditioner. I'd recently discovered that my cleaning lady, Paulina, used the same conditioner—mine. I'd been collecting evidence. There was only one conclusion: She undressed, climbed into the tub, turned on the shower, and conditioned her hair while she scrubbed the tiles.

The intimacy study was being conducted in Washington, D.C., by the world-famous marriage experts Dr. Louise Goldin Gruber, Ph.D., and Dr. Franklin Gruber, Ph.D. My editor said I had a choice. I could interview the Grubers about their research so far or I could speak to them about becoming a part of the ongoing study. "That way," she said, "you could write the story from the inside."

I felt excited about being a part of an intimacy

study. Then I felt scared. What if my husband and I had the wrong kind of intimacy?

The second I hung up I called Phoebe. She lived in Georgetown now with a second husband I'd never met. I asked her what she thought.

"Yes! You should come. You'll get to meet my cat."

"I mean, about the study."

"Why would you do that to your marriage? It's like you're being . . . you know. That word."

"Stupid?"

"No."

"Mean."

"A self word . . ."

"Involved?" I offered.

"Destructive. You're being self-destructive."

Was I? I loved my husband and my marriage. No. Privately, I worried I was something worse, something I didn't know the word for. I had once competed against Tony Randall on an afternoon game show. I honestly didn't mind sharing my feelings about insurance companies with strangers who telephoned during the dinner hour. Recently I had spent a morning with my name pinned to my chest, offering my opinions about how Bergdorf Goodman could turn itself into an even more unaffordable and luxurious store than it already was. How had this happened? My plan had been to meet middle age with exquisite dignity and chic restraint. As usual, I had veered off course. I was headed in the Dame Edna direction.

"We'd have to go to Washington," I told my husband now. "On a weekday."

"I can't take time off for something like that," he said. "And I thought you said you were finished writing articles about women."

I had said that. More than once. Step aside, I had told myself. Give women the age of the daughters you don't have a turn to write about intimacy. I liked the idea of myself stepping aside. Through this one small act I, too, could experience motherhood. I even felt a little disappointed that no one seemed to be noticing my selflessness or thanking me for it. But having stepped aside, I had no money to spend at the even more luxurious and unaffordable Bergdorf Goodman.

"I'd get to visit Phoebe," I told him. "And meet Louise Goldin Gruber."

Phoebe used to live on the inconvenient Upper West Side. Our friendship was old and complicated. And who hasn't heard of Louise Goldin Gruber? I'd once interviewed the feminist psychologist by telephone and had quoted from her many books about intimacy during my single years, when I wrote a romantic advice column for women. Many of her statements remained stuck in my mind like famous movie dialogue. "If you and your partner haven't been angry, you haven't been intimate." What intimacy actually was, though—that was something I continued to wonder. Louise Goldin Gruber's books never said. In that respect they were unlike the many fine editions of *The Joy of Cooking*, where you could always sneak a look at how to boil an egg.

Was it possible I'd once known what intimacy was

and had forgotten? Forgetting was as big among people my age as the unconscious once was. Phoebe always forgot the one word crucial to her point. My husband had celebrity Alzheimer's. He insisted that the host of *Investigative Reports* was George Peppard, no matter how many times I told him sternly, "George Peppard is dead." I remembered a prescient piece of advice my mother had given me when I was a child. "Save everything. Even hats will come back." Perhaps an answer to what intimacy was would eventually reappear, but with a little more clarity, the way a half-horrifying or almost tantalizing news fragment came back around on the TV crawl. Maybe all you could do was wait in calm hopefulness for that moment, with the help of a Xanax or some yoga if necessary, and hope that this time you'd be paying attention.

"I like being married to you," my husband said. He squeezed my hand.

"You do?" I said. I meant, Tell me more.

"What I like about being married to you," he said, "is that I can say look at that building, and you look."

What I liked was that my husband kept my hand in his when we walked, and sometimes just by the way he squeezed it I knew that he wanted me to pretend to be a prancing pony. I liked the Nodders, the couple we had invented for those times we caught ourselves wagging our heads at each other in ridiculous, sustained agreement. Was this intimacy?

"Will the magazine pay travel expenses?" he said now. I felt relieved. I remembered that my husband was willing. He was willing to please me. I didn't have to torture him with intimacy. I could go to Washington alone. I could write the article from the outside.

Penn Station was as hellish as I remembered it but had conveniently forgotten when I decided to take the train to Washington. As soon as I claimed my seat, I called Phoebe to confirm our plan. I would take a taxi to the Starbucks where the Grubers had suggested we have our conversation, and Phoebe would pick me up there later in the day.

"Are you wearing a pillbox hat?" I asked her. Phoebe was invited to a luncheon that day. It was organized around a menu Jackie Kennedy had served at the White House when she was First Lady. Apparently, that was what you did when you moved to Washington. You went to a Jackie Kennedy Reenactment Lunch.

"I can't really talk," Phoebe said in a low voice. Then in an unnaturally normal voice, "I can't wait to see you! I'll see you later." The artifice, the low talking. They indicated a husband in the room. I hung up feeling nostalgic for my mother.

I pictured Paulina entering my apartment at this moment. I was so happy not to be there. "Ajax is my friend and Pledge is my friend," Paulina insisted in her usual stubborn way whenever I bought a cleaning product made of natural ingredients like olive oil and orange. "This rag is my super-friend," she had told me more than once. Last week she had left that wet rag to dry on the metal radiator cover even though I had told her repeatedly that this caused the cover to rust. I had cracked open the window and placed the rag on the sill to dry. The next morning the rag was gone. Paulina's friend had fallen out of the window.

The train began to move, and I settled in with my book, the true story of an ill-fated love affair between the beautiful young wife of a congressman from New York City and the dashing son of Francis Scott Key. It all took place in the distant past, my favorite time. I looked out the window and was filled with contentment. I was on a train. There was no landscape, ugly or beautiful, to demand my attention. No aspiring terrorist had taken the seat next to me. None of the passengers within view were badly dressed. I had the right book with me, one about adultery and not motherhood. I was happily married but alone, nothing in the immediate past to regret, nothing in the immediate future to fear. In between—the best place to be.

By the time we pulled into Union Station, I had begun to feel anxious and unbalanced. What was it I was supposed to ask the Grubers? Why hadn't I worried about that instead of reading my book and staring blankly out the window? Once again I wondered how I had managed to succeed, or at least carve out a subsistent standard of living, in a line of work so dependent upon my least favorite thing—eliciting the views and opinions of other people. Why would anyone interesting enough to interview be interested in being interviewed by me? And if a person wasn't particularly interesting, my thinking went, why bother interviewing that person at all? Why not just elicit the views and opinions of close personal friends who were interesting? And really, why even go to that much trouble? Why not interview just one close personal friend with many interesting views and opinions? This last strategy explained how Phoebe's insights into love and marriage had come to be shared with millions of women over the years.

I hailed a taxi and told the driver the address of the Starbucks. It seemed as strange to meet in a Starbucks to talk about intimacy as it did for married psychologists to live in Washington, D.C., the capital of no-psychology. The last time I had visited Washington was during the Carter administration. The time before that I had been a child in a new spring coat. I could tell I wasn't in New York—the buildings we passed were low and decorous-looking, the avenues spacious and dignified.

That's when I asked the driver if we were anywhere near the White House. I hadn't recognized a single identifiable monument or landmark so far. It was the wrong season for cherry blossoms. "You can't drive past the White House anymore," the driver told me. I understood that by "anymore" he meant the new terrible present. "Can you still stand in front of it?" I asked him. I had looked forward to standing in front of the White House, wherever it was—not today's White House but the White House from the past. I wanted to relive the scene in my book in which the jealous congressman shoots his wife's lover. Was the past also off-limits now?

162

I was reminded of a day a few months earlier. My husband and I had driven out of the city to the farm of a midwife herbalist I was interviewing for a magazine story. It was a beautiful early fall afternoon. The midwife herbalist gave us a tour of the workroom and garden, and while my husband dozed off in the barn, demonstrated how to make facials and skin salves and answered my many questions about how valerian compared to Ambien as a sleeping aid. Then she made lunch from kale grown in the garden. Kale was a vegetable my husband could stay awake for. He praised the kale so enthusiastically that the midwife filled a bag for us to take home. We were on our way back to the city when we spotted the exit for West Point. "Would you like to see it?" my husband said eagerly.

I'd seen West Point many years before, long before I knew my husband, but I couldn't remember anything about the place. The way he said it made it sound like something I really would like to see—the pretty little cemetery in Rome, say, or the Paris atelier of Coco Chanel, or the site where Schliemann excavated Troy—and his simple enthusiasm almost convinced me it was.

Our car slowed, then stopped at the guardhouse. Did they charge admission? I dug out my wallet. Men in camouflage clothes were milling about, young men, and all of them carried rifles. I perked up. My husband lowered his window and smiled at one. "We're just here to tour the campus," he said. The young man didn't smile back. Instead he said sharply, "Go about your business, sir." We were stunned. Who would expect to encounter this rude, emergency tone of voice on an afternoon of herbal remedies and colorful foliage? Go about your business, sir. The matter-of-fact aggression of that voice, along with the rifle, indicated that we were to turn around at once and exit the way we came in. Why? The young man's handsome closed face made it clear that it was useless to ask. I scanned my husband's face to see if he felt the same guilty excitement I felt. Was this it? Had something bad happened? Was something bad about to happen? But my husband's face looked the way it always did—baffled but hopeful of a good outcome.

Just the week before the trip to West Point, I had told him I thought we should each pack a bag: cash, flashlight, medications, water, etc. In preparation, I'd already transferred a week's worth of my own sleeping pills, antidepressants, tranquilizers, and acid reflux inhibitors into one bottle. The effect was so colorful and geometrically appealing, though, I was certain Paulina would be dipping into it at any moment. She would think that the pale blue-, purple-, white-, and peach-colored pills were an advanced cosmetic treatment program.

"Hawney, bring me back French cream, for wrinkles," she had whined before a trip I'd taken to Paris two years before that. I assumed she was talking about the costly and American Crème de La Mer that Bergdorf Goodman sold on its makeup floor. Who could afford that?

"Here, use what I use—Moisturel," I said. Why not? She was already using it. "It's better than French."

My husband didn't see the point of an emergency bag. He didn't see the emergency.

"Well, let's just say there was one, for conversational purposes."

"That's what credit cards are for," he said.

Of course, if something bad had happened, what good would a packed bag have done us on the Taconic Parkway, miles from our—my—medications? No, you had to be in a safe place in order for something bad to happen—otherwise, no emergency. On that day, however, nothing bad had happened, and we continued on our way.

That was a Sunday, the changing of the guard night in our kitchen. While my husband made dinner, I watched a newsmagazine show about a suitcase a producer had filled with plutonium and sent off to travel around the world. The suitcase, taped up and homely-looking, sat in the overhead rack on a train through Romania and Bulgaria. Then it got packed inside a fancy decorative chest, nailed into a crate, and placed on a ship that sailed from Istanbul to New York City. Click, click, click. Not once did anyone demand to look inside that suitcase. Exactly, I thought. Also, how did a producer get plutonium?

The promising smell of Parmesan and garlic drifted in from the kitchen.

"What is it?" I called out, still skeptical.

"Don't worry, you'll like it," my husband called back.

Then it appeared in front of me on one of our big yellow plates. It was kale. And I did like it.

In bed that night I wound myself around my husband, displacing piles of spreadsheets. I knew I had a three-second window between Warren Buffett and irreversible coma, states as mysterious to me as Romania and Bulgaria.

There were no Grubers in Starbucks when I walked in. Then about five seconds after I got a table, there they were. Louise Goldin Gruber wore jeans and a sweater. She had long, middle-aged graduate student hair, wavy with sparks of silver and held back by a glittery barrette. She had a private smile and arresting green eyes. Franklin Gruber wore a suit. He didn't look like a therapist or an academic. I didn't know what he looked like. Then it came to me that he looked like an agent.

"Well, your persistence pays off," he had told me when I phoned to make the arrangements. I had no idea what persistence he meant. The only time I could remember my persistence paying off had involved getting tickets to see Bruce Springsteen.

"This is where you want to sit?" Franklin said when we had introduced ourselves. I realized that the look of discontent on his face was related to the coffeemaker chugging away over his shoulder.

We moved to a different table and settled in, then I got in line with the coffee orders.

I returned with two lattes, a chai tea, and a plate of heart-shaped cookies; the next day was Valentine's Day.

I took out my notebook. I realized that I was embedded in one of my worst nightmares, the one in which no amount of small talk could dispel the atmosphere of near-calamity. Could there even be the hope of small talk with people researching Non-Patriarchal Bonds of Intimacy? There couldn't be. Add to that the fact that I was me and they were a married couple—no outsider could ever hope to see over that particular wall. All in all, I might be in a Starbucks in Washington, D.C., but what was the difference between being there and being held hostage by terrorists? According to my limbic system, there was no difference. I remembered Phoebe saying that all through her childhood her mother had told her, "It's a jungle out there." When she left home she realized that all along it had been a jungle *in* there.

"My husband and I are thinking about volunteering for your study," Dame Edna said.

"You shouldn't do it," Franklin said matter-of-factly.

"But then I could write about your intimacy study from the inside." What suitcase was I trying to get into?

"Bad idea."

Louise Goldin Gruber placed a hand on her husband's arm. "We should hear what Grace has to say," she said.

There it was, that thoughtful and engaging voice. I remembered it from our telephone interview. Back then I had been asking questions for an article called "Is This Man Marriage Material?" What about a man

who isn't sure what an emotion is? had been one of
my questions. Then I described a man not unlike the
man I was then dating, my future husband, a man who
thought tired was a feeling. I had begun to ruminate
about our gathering romance, about how it didn't scare
me. Could you love a man who didn't scare you? That
was what I had wanted to know. I had been afraid that
Louise Goldin Gruber might tell me that you couldn't,
that I was in the wrong kind of love. But what was the
right kind? She was silent. I could hear her thinking.
"Well, maybe you won't get scared," she said at last.

Sitting now in Starbucks, I pictured my husband
coming home to our empty apartment. When it got too
dark to see he would turn on a single light near his
chair. Probably he would find a Clint Eastwood movie
and fall asleep in front of it. When I met my husband,
he kept a tiny black and white TV stored away in a
closet. He hauled it out for the occasional Sunday
morning news show and certain basketball playoffs.
He couldn't trust himself, he said, to watch just a
little. He was afraid he'd spend all his time watching
junky movies. I was moved by this confession. I found
it tragic that my husband was on such suspicious
terms with pleasure. I told him about self-deprivation
and how it seemed to me a flawed strategy. I used the
analogies of dieting and vaccines. I spoke to him about
the History Channel and described the way *Law &
Order* could be seen all over the planet at any hour in
the day or night. Finally, I told him that I refused to
live in a world without easy access to both Court TV

and the *E! True Hollywood Story*. My future husband
was a reasonable man, and so a normal giant television
eventually assumed its inevitable place in our joined
life. Now I felt flushed with wifely contentment when
Friday night came around and I could give up control
of the remote and kiss my husband good night. The
luxury of climbing into bed alone with a good mystery
nowhere near being solved and Clint murmuring low
from a distant room! Had I ever felt so safe? If so I
couldn't remember when. How could I ask for terror,
too? I had thought of Louise Goldin Gruber's words
many times since then. "Well, maybe you won't get
scared." They stayed stuck in my brain. Are you feeling
lucky, punk? Well, are you?

"Why don't you tell us why you and your husband
want to participate," Louise Goldin Gruber was saying.
I realized that her voice was familiar to me in another
way—from hundreds of scenes in movies and television
series, scenes in which perps were roughed up and then
smoothed over in small windowless rooms.

I explained that my husband didn't actually want
to participate in their intimacy study.

Franklin snorted.

"Do you know that I've seen my husband cry
exactly once?" Of course they didn't know. How could
they know? "It was at the end of a television movie
about a basketball team." In fact, my husband also cried
whenever he read "The Dead." What kind of trouble
was I looking for?

Franklin placed both hands flat on the table. "I

don't think you should put your marriage in jeopardy for a magazine article," he said.

In the silence that followed, we nibbled at our cookies. They were a kind I especially liked, with the pale pink icing. I felt my spirits lift just a little bit.

"Look. I think something else has to be acknowledged," Louise Goldin Gruber said then. "It's very brave of Grace to want to be a part of the study. Let's not minimize that."

We fell silent again. I began to feel a little bit heroic.

I remembered to take out my tape recorder at some point and I got the Grubers to talk about the patriarchy and how it held everyone hostage, boys and girls and men and women. By the time they were finished, I wished I could take up arms myself. Who was the patriarchy to say what a couple was, anyway? Wasn't it a fact that marriages that seemed great turned out not to be that great? It was never too late to be disillusioned on that subject. Just recently I had learned that the teenaged couples who danced on *American Bandstand* when I watched that show after school, the squiggly telephone cord my partner, weren't even real couples. Arlene and Kenny? Frani and Mike? Saying those names still evoked an intimacy of the most convincing and desirable kind. But this article had maintained they were just pretending to be couples.

"Is that someone you know?" Franklin said, frowning. He was looking out the window.

It was Phoebe, peering in. She was holding up a

cat in the same reckless way Michael Jackson held up that baby. She was making the cat wave at us. I could see that she was wearing her version of lady luncheon clothes—a nubby jacket sweater and some kind of cockeyed hat with the word "Paris" written all over it. It seemed like a bad idea for Phoebe and the Grubers to meet. Phoebe didn't believe in the patriarchy or the unconscious.

I said my goodbyes and thank-yous to the Grubers. I still felt a little sad about not being a part of the study. But then just before we separated Louise Goldin Gruber said my favorite words. "You can always change your mind. Wait and see how you feel after you write the article." I would have embraced her.

When I got into Phoebe's car, I was relieved to see that the cat was in the back seat in a carrier. Like me, Phoebe had always been a dog person. Now she had a cat she never stopped talking about. Back in college, I never could have guessed that there would be so much life ahead for Phoebe and me. There had already been enough to include a change of heart about cats. Who knew what else might happen?

We barreled out into traffic. Phoebe had an itinerary planned. That was one thing that hadn't changed.

"You have to see the Holocaust Museum and the Sargent exhibit," she said.

"I have to stand in front of the White House," I said.

"You can't come to Washington and not see the Holocaust Museum, Grace."

"I just need to stand in front it. I've never seen the Vietnam Memorial."

"Well, of course you have to see that. The White House you can see every week on that TV show."

"Maybe we should go back to your house," I told her. "I can meet Ned." And take a nap. There would be time to stand in front of the White House tomorrow.

"Ned left town this morning on business."

"I don't get to meet Ned?" That didn't sound bad. Husbands had a place in a long friendship—in the background. Later this evening I would call mine. I would probably wake him. We would have a vague, well-meant, disconnected exchange—you couldn't call it a conversation—the way we always did on the telephone. Then I would say brightly, "Okay, sweetie! I'll see you tomorrow!" I'd hang up before I killed him.

"Stop! There's the White House right there," I said. I could see it, looking exactly like itself, across a small park.

"Okay, jump out," Phoebe said. "I'll circle back around and get you on the other side of the park. But hurry. It's practically rush hour."

I did jump out. Then I walked alongside what I realized was Lafayette Square, toward Pennsylvania Avenue. Ahead of me was the corner where the enraged congressman in my book spotted his wife's lover and called out, "Key, you scoundrel, you have dishonored my home—you must die!" I stood stock-still on the sidewalk, looking around, picturing the scene. I was concentrating on pretending that it was 1859 when

I became aware that a policeman carrying a rifle was speaking to me. "Keep it moving," he said. I kept it moving, right to the other side of the square. By the time Phoebe pulled up a few moments later, the past had disappeared.

The next morning, it was after nine when I woke up in Phoebe's guest room. It was quieter here than in New York, but with the same familiar whir of Black Hawk helicopters in the background. Phoebe had left me a note saying she would pick up breakfast at the farmer's market and there was coffee in the kitchen. She had probably been up for hours, running in that park where they sometimes found bodies.

I wandered through the rooms. Each room was orderly and fresh-smelling. I could tell that Phoebe had a housekeeper whose friends were Citra-Solv and other environmentally gentle products. I imagined telling Phoebe about Paulina. It would be like admitting a bad boyfriend. It was way too late in life to have a bad boyfriend. The kitchen was particularly spotless, with enough room for two dishwashers.

In the living room, I picked up and put down objects that I recognized from Phoebe's past lives. There were photographs of Lulu: as a toddler, an impossibly beautiful teenager with silky blond hair, a law school graduate. There were watercolors Phoebe had done that I'd never seen before. I remembered that she always slept through her eight o'clock color class. "I know a lot about art, I just don't know what I like," she used to say.

The first fissure in our friendship had occurred over a married man twice my age, a war photographer. I had fallen in love with him during our first year in New York. Phoebe had disapproved. "You never used to like World War II," she said accusingly one night over dinner.

When the doorbell rang, I was examining a photograph of Phoebe's husband, Ned. I was shocked to see that, exactly our age, he looked old enough to be our father. We were old enough to be our parents.

I could see a van parked in front with the name of a florist on the side and I remembered it was Valentine's Day. I opened the door to a deliveryman smiling a smile I was pretty sure you'd have to call a grin. The flowers were for me. He reminded me of a character in a thirties screwball comedy presenting the heroine—Irene Dunne or Katharine Hepburn or Jean Arthur—with a gift she never quite expected. In a movie like that, the deliveryman would turn out to be Cary Grant or Clark Gable, and he would only be pretending to grin like a fool.

I brought the flowers into the kitchen and placed them on the counter, standing on my toes to breathe in the flower shop smell from the open top of the cellophane wrapping. My heart skipped as I unpinned the card. It was hard to remember how smart those old movies were about love. It was so long ago.

Acknowledgments

Thank you to the MacDowell Colony and the Corporation of Yaddo for their generous and timely support. David McCormick and Leslie Falk offered me the irresistible combination of exquisite sensibilities and superb counsel. My deep appreciation goes to Marysue Rucci and David Rosenthal, editor and publisher supreme, respectively, who said the single most important word: yes. Thank you to everyone at Simon & Schuster, especially Victoria Meyer, Julia Prosser, and Ginny Smith, who shepherded me into publication so gracefully.

I am blessed with friends who provided not only encouragement but also a willingness to read draft after draft (after draft), in particular Christopher Corcoran, Anita Davidson, Pam Elgar, Dalma Heyn,

Taije Silverman, Judy Stone, and Robyn Todd. I remain grateful to Beth Vesel, who planted the seed.

Jane Mankiewicz, with her fine ear and wise heart, offered me invaluable editing all the way through.

Thank you to the editors who took notice of some of these stories early on: C. Michael Curtis, Don Lee and Antonya Nelson, Joanna Yas, Pam Durban, Susan Burmeister-Brown, and Linda B. Swanson-Davies.

My largest debt of gratitude is to Philip Schultz at the Writers Studio, who showed me the way and gave me a home.

About the Author

Lesley Dormen has received fellowships from the MacDowell Colony and the Corporation of Yaddo. She lives in New York City, where she teaches fiction writing at the Writers Studio.